# MR COLLINS IN LOVE

*A Pride and Prejudice inspired m/m romance*

LEE WELCH

# CONTENTS

www.leewelchwriter.com

**Mr Collins in Love**



Edited by: May Peterson

Cover design: www.miblart.com



**ISBN:** 978-1-0670221-2-9 (Print)

# CHAPTER 1

**Note: The events in this book begin in June 1811, a few months before the events of Pride and Prejudice.**

"Good, Mr Collins," said my patroness, Lady Catherine De Bourgh. "That sounds most satisfactory."

I breathed again, murmured a thank you, and bowed over my gilt-rimmed teacup.

She took a sip of tea, nibbled her seedcake.

My detailed account of the new linen cupboards in the rectory—work she had been so gracious as to suggest herself—had gone over well. I'd barely slept the previous night, debating with myself whether she would consider my raising such a domestic detail to be an impertinence or a compliment to her wise advice. However, in the end, I had proceeded, and it was now clear I had done the right thing.

Since my account had gone so well, a repetition of the essential points might not go amiss. I have often observed that many people repeat themselves much of the time, generally to the apparent pleasure of all.

Lady Catherine and I were seated—along with Miss de Bourgh and Miss de Bourgh's companion, Mrs Jenkinson—

amidst the blue and gilt of the Rosings drawing-room, and I first attempted to ascertain from their respective demeanours whether either of those ladies wished to take their turn in the conversation.

Miss de Bourgh was gazing palely into her tea cup. Miss Jenkinson appeared to be studying, with some reverence, the lace upon Lady Catherine's dress.

I opened my mouth, therefore, to reiterate just how commodious the new arrangements for the rectory linen were, when Lady Catherine gave me a sharp assessing look, quite unlike her usual glances, which were generally so brief she barely put herself to the trouble of focusing upon me at all.

I tried not to flinch. What had I said—or not said? I schooled my expression to what I hoped was one of mild inquiry, and wished, with a part of my mind, that the room was not so stuffy and that Lady Catherine would permit a window or two to be opened.

"Yes," she proclaimed. "I have said it before and I will say it again: An establishment such as yours can never have too much storage, and shelves, I am persuaded, are of far more use than any other kind of cupboard space. Indeed, I'm certain you will be very glad of those shelves—" I opened my mouth to agree, but she went on, "—and I am sure so will your wife."

My heart dropped like a winged bird, for I had no wife.

Had she momentarily mistaken me for some other clergyman of her acquaintance? Should I correct her? Or was it more gracious to ignore her error? But then, what if she laboured under the misapprehension that I indeed had a wife for several days or weeks? At some point it must come out that I did not. All kinds of embarrassments came trumpeting towards me. I must hint at my confusion.

"W...wife, Ma'am?" I managed.

She raised her eyebrows. "Certainly. You are a single man, are you not? And in possession, now, of a very tolerable living. Not exactly a fortune, perhaps, though it might be called so by some men in your position, Mr Collins, indeed it might. So, now you must be in want of a wife."

I went hot all over. My face felt stiff and I could not blink.

I bowed again. It was difficult while seated and holding a full cup of tea, but it gave me a moment's respite from her eyes, which were pale and piercing and altogether too much. Miss de Bourgh and Mrs Jenkinson had been disturbed from their reveries and were also directing their gazes at me, clearly wondering how I would react. My mind went blank, as it did at times of strain.

My tea was quivering against the golden rim of the cup. There, a little had spilled into the saucer, leaving a stain down the outside of the cup. Bad. Must not spill any more. Nor fumble the cup and break it. Nor keel over, cup and all, onto the expensive Turkey carpet while they all stared at me in horror.

She meant I must *get* a wife. That I must marry.

If only one could anticipate such outrageous topics. If only one had time to prepare a suitable response. But I had no time, and anyway, I knew what was expected.

"Just...just so, Ma'am," I managed. "Your ladyship is quite right, I am sure."

I risked a glance. Her visage, never encouraging, had become stony, nostrils slightly flared. I had not agreed with sufficient celerity. She put down her morsel of seedcake.

Silence was descending upon me; that unhappy state, almost of paralysis, that has oft afflicted me in company since childhood. My tongue was made of lead, my mind as quick as a lump of clay.

Once I should have remained thus; speechless, staring, almost deaf. These days, I knew what to do: I must become Trafford.

Trafford. His very name was a magic spell. Already my tongue felt lighter, my mind less dull.

Trafford, the son of a bishop. Trafford, whom I had never met but whom I had observed so many times at Oxford. His borrowed consequence and loquacity had saved me a thousand times. Aping Trafford had got me my current position. It had helped me keep my patroness's good opinion these several months.

I pictured him, now, at table in the hall, surrounded by men of his acquaintance, words dancing from his lips in a ceaseless rivulet. I sat straighter. Yes, I was Trafford. Full of talk and opinion, all of it suitable, all of it expressing the right opinions and the correct preferences of a clergyman. I cleared my throat.

"As your ladyship so wisely points out, matrimony is a blessed institution, and one that those members of the clergy for whom it may be possible must certainly enter into if they are fortunate enough to find themselves in a position to do so."

I had only just begun, but Lady Catherine, who was eyeing her cake as if it were a slug upon her plate, interrupted.

"Yes, Mr. Collins, but I do not make this observation in general terms. Indeed, I have given the matter some thought and I see no reason for you to delay. You are five-and-twenty, are you not? That is *quite* old enough for marriage." She lifted a hand as if I had tried to interject. "Gentlemen of leisure may marry when they please—though what they hope to gain by delaying overlong *I* fail to comprehend—but you are not a gentleman of leisure. You are the rector of Hunsford and as such you must consider your position and the duties incumbent upon you."

I opened my mouth to say that I *did* consider my position, that I considered it almost every waking hour and often at night too, and that I took my duties very seriously indeed, but she was speaking again.

"A wife will greatly assist you in those duties. I am an observant person, as you know, and I have often remarked that a parson's wife may facilitate any number of small matters about the parish." She picked up her cake and added, "Beef tea. Baskets. And so on." She took a bite of cake.

I wanted to say that if it were truly a matter of facilitating my duties, what I really needed was a new cob, because Pilot was lame again, and in the matter of saving shoe leather, a new horse would be a great deal more use than a wife. But I realised, just in time, that a new cob could not make beef tea, and that in any case Lady Catherine likely was not truly interested in facilitating my duties. She wished me to marry for reasons of her own—because she thought it fitting, or to prove to herself the degree of control she had over me, or perhaps simply because a clergyman's wife may be counted upon to make up the numbers at quadrille when there is no better company to be had.

"Quite so, Ma'am," I murmured. "Beef tea. Quite so."

Lady Catherine nodded. "Moreover, the parsonage is well appointed—" She cocked her head, as if considering just *how* well appointed. I winced internally, for I was conscious of the great comfort in which I lived, my father having taught me well to both crave luxury and to feel guilty about enjoying it.

"—*very* well appointed," Lady Catherine was saying. "*Some* might consider it now almost *too* well appointed for a clergyman, though I'm sure I should not concern myself with such quibbling."

It was a threat, of course. I can be stupid when it comes to conversation, but I am good at recognising threats, having become accustomed over the years.

Lady Catherine glanced around the drawing-room, as if daring us to leap up and contradict her.

Miss de Bourgh murmured, "No, Ma'am," and Mrs Jenkinson did likewise. I joined them; an echo of an echo. Polite demurrals seemed to linger always in that drawing-room, caught in the very upholstery like the grubs of moths.

Lady Catherine inclined her head, mollified by our chorus, but the steely glint in her eye remained. "Very well, then. It is settled. Mr. Collins, you are to marry. I am sure you will not disappoint me."

"No, Ma'am."

I hoped that was an end to the matter, for my hands were shaking and my stomach cramping around the mouthful of tea and the bite of cake I had consumed. But when I dared to glance up, she was still watching me in that new and unnerving manner, sparse eyebrows raised in mild expectation.

I added, "I'm sure I hope I should never do that. Indeed, when your ladyship has bestowed such unlooked-for generosity upon her humble servant, I should be mortified to cause even an ounce of disappointment."

I spoke fluently enough and allowed myself a moment of pride at being able to speak at all. My Trafford trick was clever, indeed it was. But my heart was sunk to my lights, for I could see there would be no escaping this most unpleasant of circumstances.

Lady Catherine moved on to other topics. I nodded, tutted, murmured a word of praise or censure, added a suitable allusion, now Biblical, now classical, and generally did all I could to comport myself as the rector of Hunsford. I felt, however, as a boy awaiting a beating. It was only the company that stopped a tear from escaping my eye. I did not want to marry. I had no interest whatsoever in such an adventure, for reasons both personal and private.

But now I must find a suitable woman. Respectable, but not too fine. I must woo her. That meant dancing, alas. Making conversation, more was the pity. Praise of her more amiable qualities. Well, the latter I could do. I was accustomed to thinking up little compliments to try to please the ladies.

Then I must tell her I wished to make her my wife.

Wait.

First, I must assure her of my high esteem and most tender feelings. Yes, that was expected. *Then* I must tell her I wished her to be my wife.

I must marry her. Then I must lie with her, more than once, though I was uncertain how often was considered proper. Elegant females did not speak of such things and so perhaps did not have great expectations in that area. Indeed, perhaps they preferred husbands who did not make many demands of that type? Ah, but women expected children, did they not? So, it would likely be necessary to lie with her until she'd had at least one child, or probably three or four.

And then—upon my word, but the horror was coming ever clearer!—she would have opinions. She would have preferences. She would invite company beyond what was necessary. She might want alteration in my little household. She might want me to turn off Mrs Fowke, my housekeeper. She might dislike Milly, the maid. She might say that old George, Mrs Fowke's brother, was too infirm to dig the garden and tend the animals.

I wanted no change to anything. Mrs Fowke was a kindly, bustling sort who made excellent suet puddings and boiled her potatoes to a nicety; never too much, never too little. Milly was quiet, middle-aged, untroublesome. Perhaps there was sometimes dust upon the window ledges but that mattered not since she neither sang nor clattered as she went about her business. No, I must not lose Milly.

And George—it was true he suffered from his rheumatics very severely sometimes and that he was prone to agues besides, but if that meant I had to do a little extra, well, I *liked* working in the garden. I enjoyed it above all things. And he was not terrifying in the manner of so many gardeners of my acquaintance. I did not have to gird my loins to give him a simple direction about the leeks. He had never once glowered or sulked.

A wife could ruin it all. She might want me to get a new man. A carriage. Fancy things from London. She would fuss and make alterations and say things wouldn't do. And I should have to listen to her and do as she said, for a man is a tyrant if he does not listen to his wife and the rector of Hunsford must set a good example.

Yet I could not refuse Lady Catherine. A few short months ago I had expected to remain a curate all my life, or at least for decades, until Mr Bennet died and I could inherit Longbourn. Being given the living at Hunsford was the type of good fortune that came but once a lifetime. I owed my patroness everything.

I took my leave at six o'clock and walked home through Rosings Park. It was Sunday evening, usually the best part of the week with my duty done for the day. The park was glorious, the sunlight slanting green and gold through the summer trees, but I could not enjoy it. Instead, I must consider the young females of my acquaintance with a view to matrimonial suitability.

There was Miss Cowper. She had a kind smile and was pleasant to behold. But she was surely too fine, and anyway, was there not talk of an understanding with Captain Harvey?

There was Miss Cook, but she was too giddy for a rector's wife. She was loud besides, with a clear, carrying voice and a laugh that set my teeth on edge.

There was Miss Norris. She spoke soft and never raised her eyes. She would make no demands upon me, I was bound, nor insist upon my hiring a new housekeeper or a new man. But she must be five-and-thirty, at least. Lady Catherine would never approve my marrying such an old maid.

There were Miss Polkington and her sisters; Miss Henrietta, Miss Emma and Miss Patricia. They were gentlewomen with no fortunes. One of them would doubtless be glad to say yes to their young rector. Only they did titter so, and had such a quantity of aunts, all of whom would doubtless insist upon visiting very regularly. My long peaceful evenings would be quite at an end.

Perhaps a lady from further afield who had not so many relations in Kent?

Before Lady Catherine had bestowed the living upon me, I had been curate to a Mr Clarke, in Sussex, not far from where I had grown up. He had three daughters. They had laughed at me behind my back and sometimes played me tricks, stuffing paper in my hatband and salting my tea, but perhaps they would be kinder now I was in a position to marry? Mr Clarke had not been my friend, exactly, and could be rather terse, but he would not likely gainsay me a visit.

Yet I saw in my mind's eye the pretty faces of his daughters, arrayed about the dining table like flowers, ringlets shaking and eyes bright with silent derision as they glanced at one another and then at me.

I kicked at a nettle at the side of the path.

Cats. Those Clarke girls were little cats.

Or no, because that was unfair to domestic felines, who had ever been sweeter to me than they.

I am not easily angered or offended. I know my shortcomings too well. I am no wit, no sportsman. I am pleasing neither in person nor in conversation. But I had really done my utmost with the Misses Clarke. I had tried always to be pleasant and polite. I had prepared little compliments and spoken no words but of praise. I had attempted to model my conduct upon that of the local squire's son, a gentleman whom the Misses Clarke had professed to esteem most highly.

I took a deep breath and unclenched my fists. I had not noticed that I had clenched them but recalling the Misses Clarke did that to me. Well, doubtless, my anger was unwarranted. Likely, I was the one at fault. All the same, I should not look to Sussex for a wife.

If only I knew a sympathetic fellow with whom I could discuss this matter of finding a wife, as honestly as decency would allow. Yet I had ever struggled to make acquaintances. I had but one friend in my youth, and Jem was a common farm labourer's son and long lost to me besides.

A sweet ache arose in my chest, as it did when I thought of Jem and his preferment of me. I had been afraid of him at first due to his large size, his beetling brow and hare lip, all of which had given him a fearsome aspect. But I had soon learned that for all his brawn he was mild and gentle, kind to wild things and upset by strife or raised voices. Once I had got to know him, I had privately sometimes fancied him kin to the giant, feather-hocked horses his father had once worked with on the farm; so strong he had no need to prove it.

We had not talked much, Jem and I. He had been my father's

gardener's boy and had perforce many duties to attend to. It had been enough that he had sometimes joined me on my rambles about the woods and the levels, that he had let his shoulder rest against mine when we sat side by side, and that he had seemed to take it for granted that we should share whatever we had, whether it was my hatful of blackberries or his crust of bread.

The year we turned fifteen we had shared some other things besides, but then I had been sent away to school and when I had returned at the end of that dreadful first term, he had run away to sea. I had never seen him again.

I passed beneath the great oak, which stood in my favourite section of the park, but even the proximity of that gracious giant could not cheer me today. The path dipped through a coppice of sweet chestnut, and there, across the little footbridge, was the rectory. *My* rectory. I had dwelt there since Easter and it was but June, but had I lived there all my life, and my forebears before me, I could not have loved it more.

It was a solid square building of grey stone, with two storeys and some garret rooms above for the servants. It had a neat, dependable, well-appointed aspect. The flower garden was a riot of colour, with roses and honeysuckle, celandine, lavender, pansies and eglantine. There was an orchard behind, with damsons, apples, pears and cherries, as well as a mulberry tree and a nuttery with a spreading walnut, white filberts, hazels and cobnuts. Beyond that, my glebe lands; two fine pastures with sheep, half a dozen cows, and some pigs.

I passed the profusion of raspberry canes and gooseberry bushes, and the vegetable garden with its rows of carrots, beans, onions, leeks, potatoes and marrows. Many of these I had planted myself and, despite my current dilemma, it gave me a thrill to see those rows burgeoning. There were the herbs; the lovage and the fennel, the mint, marjoram and thyme. The drone of the dumbledores grew loud and the air was shot with gold.

Perhaps I could find a wife who would understand that

nothing must be changed? Who would see that my folk must not be upset and made to do anything differently?

I sighed. That did not seem likely.

Some people, I am persuaded, are made for happiness. They understand how to enjoy and to husband it. Since my first bewildered week at Hunsford, when I had walked about in a daze, I had suspected something terrible would happen to rob me of it. I had ever felt like a child with a honeycomb who has just kicked the hive. He can feel his happiness. He can, perhaps, even taste it, but he knows that in a moment it will be gone.

I squared my shoulders. To expect happiness in life is to be fortunate indeed. Even if I married, I would still have the living. I would still be the rector. I would have that, most likely, until I died, unless I disgraced myself in some truly ghastly manner.

Even with a shrewish wife, I would have my study with the window that opened onto the lilacs, and I would have my garden and the song of the bees and my walks in Rosings Park. And if my wife despised me then I should endure it, as I had endured life before Hunsford, with as much patience and courage as I could muster.

Mrs Fowke came hurrying towards me from behind the house. Her hair was escaping her cap and she was red-faced and frowning. She carried a colander and must have been on her way to the vegetable garden. Picking vegetables wasn't usually her job, so likely George was poorly again. She was probably worried about him, hence her expression, which was usually more pacific.

I greeted her, and she bobbed a curtsey.

"Oh, Mr Collins, there you are, sir. Oh, sir, I must tell you. George is taken bad again and there's been a foreigner in the lane all afternoon. And he hasn't come to the door, and he hasn't gone away, and Mr Butler came by in his gig and we thought that had scared him off, but Milly saw him again not half an hour since and he's after our fowl, I'll be bound."

I could not understand her alarm, for foreigners, as she called them, came regularly to Kent. They were Londoners, generally, looking for work on the farms. I wanted to get to my study and find a piece of sermon paper and list the names of the ladies I had considered so far. Two lists, actually: 'Suitable' and 'Unsuitable'. I did not want to forget anyone for the Unsuitable list.

"Probably he is merely looking for work, Mrs Fowke," I said.

"But it ain't time, sir, begging your pardon. The planting's done and the hay in, and the hops not ripe for weeks. And he was a big-looking ruffian and all. Very ragged."

I could feel no true alarm, even though the rectory was at the far end of the village and if George was in his bed, there was nobody about but the women. "Very well. I'll go and see."

I went around the house, stopping in at the front door to get my stick from the hall table. If there was some wayfaring fellow about, twopence would probably do more good, and this I had in my pocket, but my stick made it clear to Mrs Fowke that I was taking the matter seriously.

The lane was empty in both directions, the hedgerows dreaming in the late afternoon sun. Butterflies hovered about the meadowsweet. Finches peeped and fluttered. Velvety dust arose about my ankles from the road, so white my father, had he been alive, might have used it to powder his wig.

"I see no one," I said.

Perhaps the demure Miss Norris was not yet five-and-thirty. Perhaps she was but four-and-thirty. Or three-and-thirty. It really was impossible to say. Perhaps even if she was five-and-thirty that was not, in fact, too old.

"He were there, sir." Mrs Fowke pointed left. "Towards the village. Idling in the lane, at first, and then Milly saw him in Butler's coppice. There at the edge."

I made my way along the lane, Mrs Fowke behind me, and peered into the green depths of the coppice. No dark figure lurked there.

"I think he must have gone, Mrs Fowke."

Many men married women older than themselves. Perhaps I

should make a third list, titled 'Neither Suitable Nor Unsuitable'. Miss Norris would be the first name on that list.

"Hiding, likely," Mrs Fowke said in my ear. "Anyway, I got the fowl in, just in case."

"A wise precaution."

I stepped across the tangle of weeds and wildflowers in the ditch and into the coppice. It had perhaps ten years of growth and while it was easy to walk between the trees, it would be difficult to find anyone in its depths for it was thick and covered a large area.

I cast about, startling a blackbird which flew off, disturbing the peace with its cry of alarm. I knew the coppice well for Mr Butler did not object to his neighbours walking there, but I could see nothing amiss. No ruffians lurking in the undergrowth, only foxgloves. I made my way back to the lane where Mrs Fowke stood hugging her empty colander in the sunshine, her brow knitted in concern.

"No one is there," I said. "Likely he was just some poor fellow stopping to rest in the heat of the day. I expect he has gone on now."

"If you say so, sir." She bobbed another curtsey. "I hope you'll excuse me, sir. I'm not usually one to take on, as I hope you know, only what with George taken bad...and the fellow's manner *was* odd sir, all ducking and diving like he didn't want to be—" Her eyes went round. She was staring past me, into the coppice. "Oh, sir. Oh, lawks. It's *him*."

I turned. A huge shape was emerging from the shadows. A man dressed almost in rags, his trousers gone at the knees and his jacket ripped at the shoulders. For so large a fellow he moved very silent and at the edge of the lane he stopped, several paces from us, shoulders hunched, head ducked.

He wrung a cap between hands like hams, his knuckles all scraped and scabbed. His brow was dark and heavy, and his eyes, when he glanced up, small and apologetic. He had a hare lip so that a chink of white tooth showed through as though he wore a permanent snarl.

My mouth fell open.

It could not be.

He was changed, of course. He was older. His cheeks had hollowed and had a scruffy beard. He had got a filthy blue neckerchief. But the biggest change was in his manner. He had never been one to put himself forward, but now he cringed like a man trying to hide.

*What has happened to you?* I wanted to say.

Because it was him. It was Jem. Jem Binns.

My only friend. Come back to me.

# CHAPTER 2

"Jem!" I sprang forward. "Upon my word! Is it really you?"

My arms had gone out to embrace him, but Mrs Fowke was watching and anyway he had never liked to be touched. I stopped short and held up my hands in what I hoped was a welcoming gesture suitable for the rector of Hunsford.

"Jem!" I repeated for the wonder of saying his name. "Why, it has been ten years since I saw you last. How did you get here? What brings you here?"

He blushed, ducking his head and touching his forelock, and mumbling, "Master William, sir. Beg pardon, sir, for intruding. Right good to see you, sir."

His voice was low and I remembered that he ever spoke quietly in company because his lip caused him to form words in a particular way and he was shy because of it. But his tone was so familiar that we were suddenly ten years old, crouched behind the laurels eating stolen raspberries from his hand. I could almost taste them, warm as embers, sweet as honey.

"And...are you well?" I said. "Is everything all right at home? I mean, your sister? Your brothers? Are they well? You have not brought bad news, I hope?"

"They're well, thank you, sir, as far as I know."

"Good, good. That is excellent news. Good news is so much more pleasant than bad, is it not? I am relieved, Jem. Much relieved. I was in Marshing, you know, visiting my great aunt not six weeks since. I asked after you. I asked your sister. I went to her house, particularly to ask. She said you were at sea."

"Yessir, thank you for asking after me, sir. And so I was, sir."

He would not look at me, but there was the scar on his wrist that he had got when the mattock fell upon it. His hair, which was dark brown, had ever grown low over his forehead in exactly the way it did now, and the way he towered above me so I must look up was likewise the same.

I wanted to touch him to make sure he was real. I wanted to stare at him. I could have stood in the lane staring for an hour or more. But certain things were expected of me. If he had walked from Marshing, he must be tired. Hungry.

"Well, Jem, I am very happy to see you. Very happy indeed. Will you not come and have something to eat? You must be hungry. Are you hungry?"

The first raspberries were ripe now, in my garden, and there was no one to beat us if we ate them from his hand, but we were men now and there were worse punishments than a beating. A man in my position may not gobble raspberries with the fellow who used to be his father's gardener's boy.

The raspberries were how I had met him. I had been hungry. I had always been hungry in those days. Jem had said it would be all right, that no one should catch us. His hand had been dirty and the raspberries the size of walnuts, red as fairy lanterns. Afterwards, he had licked his fingertips and rubbed juice from my cheek and sucked his fingers clean. He had seemed a part of the garden's largesse, so natural and generous. His eyes were small and of no colour or perhaps every colour, being sometimes brown and sometimes green and sometimes grey. He had smiled and said, "don't eat no more today and we won't get caught, see," and his breath had been fragrant from the fruit. I suppose I had agreed because he had said, "friends then, now, ain't we?" and his words had gone straight to my heart and lodged there, because he had never betrayed them. I had never heard the sentiment from any other person, but I had heard it from him that green summer afternoon in the secret place behind the raspberry canes.

I wanted to pull him into the coppice and run and run until we were alone, as we might have done when we were boys.

Instead, I turned to Mrs Fowke. She had her hands on her hips, the colander dangling like a saddlebag. "Mrs Fowke will find you something to eat, won't you Mrs Fowke?"

She wasn't smiling, but she wasn't angry. It was part of a clergyman's job to be charitable with food and drink and she knew it. "Course, sir. I'll be bound it's hungry work idling in our lane all afternoon."

"This is Jem...that is, Jeremiah Binns, Mrs Fowke." *He is my old friend*, was the phrase upon my lips, and perhaps I could say it, but perhaps it wouldn't be fitting. "I have known him since boyhood when he worked for my father."

"Ain't that nice then, to see a familiar face," she said.

She had often before struck me as possessing a peculiar simple wisdom, for the word 'familiar' rang in my heart like a bell. She was quite right, though I had not realised it until that moment. Hunsford was so *new* and while it was my great good fortune to be there, new situations, new people and new places have ever been trying to me. Jem was the same old Jem. He looked like home.

"Yes, yes, indeed it *is* nice to see a familiar face. It is indeed, Mrs Fowke. You are quite right."

She turned to Jem and I could see in her expression that she was forgiving him for having frightened her. "Come with me, then, lad. 'Spect you could get outside of a bit of mutton, eh?"

"Thank you, missus," Jem said humbly, ducking his head and twisting his cap so I thought he should twist it in two. But then, Mrs Fowke was a stranger to him, and I had never seen him with a stranger before. Almost everyone in Marshing had known him since birth.

Mrs Fowke turned and walked towards the rectory. Jem followed. His boots were falling apart and he was footsore, limping like old Pilot. When I visited Marshing, I rode, and stayed overnight on the way at the White Hart besides. Likely it had taken Jem three days to come this far from there. Sailors on leave were famously incontinent with their pay, but he did not look like a sailor on leave. He looked like a vagrant, and certainly could not have stretched to inns, even if one would have had him.

"But, Jem, what brings you here?" I asked.

He went a delicate shade of pink and mumbled something I could not hear.

It did not matter why he had come. My heart was beating wildly that he was here. I did not want him to feel like a stranger, yet having never been to Hunsford, he would not be cognisant of the salient features of the area. I began to point them out, my heart bubbling over with pride and pleasure at being able to show them to him.

The spine of the Weald ran over in that direction. Tonbridge was that way and Bromley the other. This was the stable gate, and over there my garden gate, that the direction of Rosings, the upper storey of which we could glimpse through the trees of the park. Here was the rectory and over there the roofs of barn and stable. My sheep were over there, as were the pigs, though he could not see them from here. Those tree tops were in a sort of wilderness that followed the line of a stream.

We reached the house and Mrs Fowke made to lead Jem around the back to the kitchen door. I had scarce set foot in the kitchen since I had arrived at Hunsford. Could a rector sit in his kitchen with his housekeeper and his maid of all work and entertain a man like Jem and watch him eat a plate of mutton?

Jem glanced at me and ducked his head again in what seemed a farewell.

No, I could not follow.

"Let us talk again when you have eaten," I called.

He nodded and disappeared around the side of the house.

My hands were trembling as I went in the front door, took off my hat and put it on the hall table, trying to reassure myself I had done nothing vulgar nor unsuitable. I had been friendly but not overly effusive. I had been familiar, but had not lowered myself. I had allowed myself to show my true sentiments, but had kept myself in check in front of Mrs Fowke. Surely, I had conducted myself quite well?

Yes, except for that last 'let's talk when you have eaten'. That, in hindsight, had been unnecessary, for it was likely obvious Jem and I should speak again once he had eaten. My cheeks grew warm, though I was alone and unobserved. I had mostly been educated at home by my father, but I had spent two years at prep school and there I had acquired the nickname 'Obvious Collins' or sometimes 'Old Obvious'. It had not been a friendly sobriquet. It was vexing, they had told me, to appraise people of facts of which they were already cognisant. In truth I had never meant to annoy anyone, merely to give voice to my understanding of whatever situation was at hand to ensure there was no confusion, for I had found the ways of the other boys so bewildering as to be quite terrifying. Perhaps if my father had sent me to school earlier, I should have known more and done better, but he had not, and in any case, it was just as likely that by educating me at home he had saved me years of torment.

Usually, these days, I was better at censuring myself, but in all the excitement, I had forgotten. It was possible they were laughing at me now in the kitchen, though, on balance, they probably were not. Servants, I had observed, generally forgave eccentricity because they had no choice and wished to keep their positions, and I had never heard Jem laughing at anyone, or at least not in an unkind manner.

Mrs Fowke would be giving him some mutton. Now, a hunk of bread, or maybe a huffkin. She would be watching him eat it.

She liked people who appreciated her food, or so she often said. I hoped Jem would not be too shy to thank her, nor to tell her how good it all was.

Now she might be giving him a draught of beer. Now, perhaps, a pickled onion.

I could not linger in the hall all evening. Where should I await my interview with Jem? My study would be the most natural place, for that was where I usually spent my evenings. But perhaps, since Jem was so dusty and ragged, the stable yard would be considered more fitting. Really, though, I longed to show him the garden.

It would soon be all over the parish that Mr Collins had given charity to a ragged fellow he had known as a boy from miles and miles away, on the south coast. All the details of the encounter would be laid out and pored over, and if I talked to Jem in my study, and people did not consider that right, they would never forget it.

Some men would have known which location was the most suitable. Trafford would have known. He would not have had to think about it. He would have met Jem in just the right place and it would all have been easy and natural.

I went to my study. The air was hot and stale and as I opened the casement, I found I still carried my stick. I returned to the front door and deposited it on the hall table.

Now, Jem would be drinking his beer. Mrs Fowke might be giving him a piece of the apple pie I sometimes ate myself after dinner. It was good pie, flavoured with nutmeg, but not too much. She served it with cream. I hoped he enjoyed it.

I went back to my study and sat at my desk. The latest issue of the *Farmer's Magazine* lay upon it. I had recently started taking it so that I might apprise myself of developments in the agricultural world and thus become a more adept conversationalist for my new neighbours. I opened the magazine and leafed through a few pages. Then I closed it and arose. If Jem was brought in, he would have to stand and I did not want that expanse of desk between us.

I seated myself in the easy chair by the grate, but it was not the same without a fire, and of course it was too warm to want one. It was a shame Jem could not have arrived in April when I should have had a fire in here, and then it would have seemed most natural and fitting to talk before the fire.

I stood up.

I should stifle in the study. Fitting or not, I must have air.

I went into the garden to look at the beans.

# CHAPTER 3

Once in the garden, though, I realised that since I usually spent Sunday evenings in my study, that was where Mrs Fowke or Milly would look for me. What if they did not think to find me in the garden? What if they let Jem go without his seeing me again? But I had said 'let's talk when you have eaten', which made it plain I expected to speak with Jem again. I was suddenly not sorry for having said it.

I looked the beans without seeing them.

Perhaps, under the circumstances, it would not be wrong for me to stop by the kitchen door? I could say 'Come, Jem, let us talk now, then I must get to my study'. Or I could invent a need for tea, or bread and butter, or some other excuse that would give me a reason to stop by the kitchen.

Then I hit upon it. The gate.

There were two front gates to the property: the main—or garden—gate and the stable gate, but both gave directly onto the lane. Jem must pass through one or the other to leave. It was more likely he would leave by the stable gate, because that would be more fitting for a man of his station, and because it lay closer to Hunsford which was likely the direction he would go when he departed. In the other direction lay only Rosings Park and some of Mr Butler's fields, and it was unlikely Jem could have any reason to go to either of those places.

I went around to the front of the house, passed alongside it and thence into the stable yard, which was some thirty yards from the house. I rested my hand upon the stable gate and at once felt easier.

Jem did not come and I began to walk to and fro. I could hear faint voices, occasionally, from around the back of the house. Mrs Fowke's, mainly, and occasionally Milly's. I could not hear Jem, but then he always spoke soft. The voices of the others seemed quite loud. They must have the kitchen door open to let in the cooler air. Or perhaps Mrs Fowke had asked him to stand outside so as to keep the kitchen clean.

Pilot stuck his head out of his box and nickered, his brown coat lit to a lovely coppery-red by the late sun. I scratched the place beneath his forelock, as he liked, and he mouthed my ear with velvet lips.

"Jem has come," I whispered to him, for the pleasure of saying it aloud. "My friend, Jem."

My eyes filled with tears as I spoke, and I wiped them away, unsure what sentiment had caused them, whether joy or relief or fear of something I could not name. Pilot rubbed his nose against my hair. How much better are beasts than humanity? Pilot listened and seemed to understand but did not remark nor try to make me explain myself. I scratched beneath his forelock again.

The house and stable faced south and the sun, though it was now low in the sky, still held a great deal of warmth. There was a bench by the stable, and I sat upon it, but the sun dazzled me and sweat pricked out under my arms and down my back. I pulled out my handkerchief and mopped my brow. Pilot blew a sweet-smelling gust through his nose and turned back to his hay net. I could get inside his stall and be out of the sun, but then I might miss Jem.

I stood up and spied a long strip of shadow under the

hedgerow on the other side of the lane. It would be cooler there. I opened the gate, crossed the lane, and edged into the shade.

The hedgerow was not quite high enough and my head and shoulders were still full in the sun. I could not sit in the dust of the road, but I stepped across the ditch and up onto the verge, which rose a little above the level of the lane at that point. I turned and stood in the long grass. Now I was in the shade of the hedge and, moreover, from my vantage point had an excellent view of the house and both gates. There was even a breeze coming through the hedgerow, pleasantly cool upon my back.

Now I could not miss him.

I had asked him why he had come and had not heard his answer. I should have begged his pardon and asked him to repeat himself, but in my excitement to show him all the points of interest I had quite failed to do so.

It seemed odd that he should come all this way to see me just because I had enquired after him at his sister's. I always enquired after him when I was in Marshing visiting my great aunt, and he had never come before. Of course, he had been at sea.

I had wondered about it earlier, but it struck me suddenly as tremendously odd that he had been dressed in rags. He must have left his ship, but why would he exchange his sailor's rig for something worse? Perhaps he had fallen on hard times, in which case he had come a long way for a few words and a bite of mutton. I was pleased, of course, but why should he—

Oh.

Money.

He must want some.

A pang that was sharper than disappointment shot through my heart. But after all, was I not likely the only person he could ask? He could not ask the new man at Marshing. The living there was very poor, as I knew well, my father having been the perpetual curate.

No, I was not disappointed. I was pleased. Of course, Jem

should come to me. Yes, I was pleased and would be gratified to be able to help him. People expected charity from a clergyman. It was fitting. Though I must not get a reputation as too soft a touch. Already I had been warned by certain farmers of my acquaintance that other farmers were ever looking for ways to give the rector rather less than one in ten come tithing time.

Anyway, when it came to Jem, it would not really be charity. Others could call it that if they wished. To me, secretly, it would be upholding the bond of friendship. Not only would I give him whatever he needed, I would not quibble nor delay but give him it immediately so he should not be embarrassed.

My noble thoughts had distracted me, and I became suddenly aware that Mrs Fowke and Jem were standing at the stable gate, peering up at me. My heart leapt to see his familiar countenance once more.

As a boy, people had called him ugly. Mr Scatcherd, my father's gardener, had called him a little old gargoyle. But to me, Jem's countenance was pleasing above all others. His dark brows were glossy as chestnuts, his eyes were kind, and his lip was charming because it was his own.

"Is...er...now convenient, sir?" Mrs Fowke sounded uncertain. "You did say as how you wanted to speak with the lad."

"Yes, yes. Thank you, Mrs Fowke." I stepped down off the verge and across the ditch. "Now will do very well. No time like the present, eh?"

She nodded and bobbed, gave the place I had been standing a puzzled glance, and went off towards the house.

I had him all to myself at the gate.

"Well, Jem!" I said. "Have you eaten? Have you had enough?"

"Yes, sir. Thank you, sir."

I did not want his thanks. As boys we had shared everything, half and half, and had taken it for granted that it should be so, or at least I had. And soon he would be going, with nothing but politeness between us.

"No, no. You are welcome." I wanted to plead with him. *Don't you remember? What's mine is yours.* But ten years had passed so I mumbled something about duty, and added, "Mrs Fowke keeps a good kitchen. We are very fortunate here."

"Yes." He twisted his cap and added, shyly, staring at his boots, "I hope it ain't getting above myself, sir, to offer my congratulations on your position here."

"Thank you, Jem. That's very kind."

"Always knew as how you'd do well, Master Willie. You being so clever, sir, with your Latin and your Greek."

In fact, I had never been much of a scholar and had got my degree by the skin of my teeth, but I was happy to hear him say the old familiar name he used to call me, and it was pleasing to be thought book-learned.

Compared to him, I suppose I was. He had never mastered his letters. I had tried to teach him myself once, but he never could seem to tell b from d and so we had not got very far. It was strange, for he was clever enough in all other respects.

"Thank you, Jem," I said. "It was great good fortune that brought me here. My previous position as a curate was much less comfortable, but I thank God for it because through it I met my esteemed patroness, Lady Catherine de Bourgh. I owe her my position here, and my happiness."

"Must be a fine lady, sir."

"Indeed, she is. I have never met a lady so high who is so gracious in her manner. Why, only the other day—well, it was perhaps three weeks ago—she praised my sermon freely."

"Yes, sir."

He looked suitably awestruck and I refrained from adding that she terrified me. Jem was no gossip and knew nobody hereabouts, but an ill-chosen word may be passed about and where it might end up one never knew.

On my first day in the rectory, I had made a solemn vow that I should never, by word or deed, in private or in public, show one single ounce of ingratitude to Lady Catherine, so that if any were ever to carry report of me to her, she should hear only humble praise and admiration. It was a good vow. It made me feel safe.

"And, you, Jem? How has life treated you?"

"Well, sir, you know I went away to sea. But it's a hard life aboard, that it is, sir. So, I came ashore last time we made port and I worked awhile in...in a tannery. Near Hastings. But I don't know as how I was suited to the work. And I...I had a wish to pay my respects and offer my congratulations. Everyone in Marshing says as how you've done so well, sir, begging your pardon."

"Thank you, Jem." I have been told my voice can be monotonous which can cause people to believe me lacking in feeling, so I tried to put true sentiment into my tone. "I am glad you came. Truly glad, for I have often thought of you and wondered how you were faring."

"Thank you, sir."

"We have both been out in the world these ten years," I added. Obvious. Bad.

"Aye, sir, that's true. Long time, ain't it?"

"Yes, it *is* a long time. We are men now, are we not?"

"Aye, sir."

He gave me a curious look. I thought he would speak more but he did not. Bees buzzed sleepily in the dog-rose that grew about the stable fence and in the scarlet geraniums that glowed in the pot by the water trough. Somewhere off in the coppice, a nightingale sang.

Now we had caught up with our news, so to speak, I thought his next words would be about money. But he did not seem to know how to ask. He simply stood there, so red in the face he put the geraniums to shame, twisting his cap almost apart.

I understood his reluctance, for I was familiar with his situation. One longs to ask—for bread or money or a friend—and yet one cannot. It is not pride, exactly, or not pride alone. It is the knowledge that, afterwards, they will know you are a person who had to ask, and they could use that information against you, if they wished.

I should have to help him.

"Jem." I used the gentlest tone I could muster. "Do you remember the day we went to Branley Chase and I fell in the eel pond. We were ten, I think. Or perhaps eleven. Do you remember?"

He glanced up, a smile lighting his eyes and lifting his heavy brows. "I do! It were that cold! And you slipped into that pond like a duckling."

"I was too afraid to go home afterwards, remember? Because I was so wet."

"Ah. Your Pa would have made a hem stink." He frowned, remembering. "Where did we go? Weren't the old boat shed. Happen it were Ilford's byre?"

"Behind it, I think. And you made a fire so I could dry my jacket."

"You were that cold you couldn't talk. Your lips were blue. Like a dead man."

"I wore your jacket while we waited. Remember?"

"And soon I couldn't talk either." He chattered his teeth and rubbed his arms in mimicry, smiling there in the summer heat. "Thought we should both catch our deaths."

"So did I. But do you remember, Jem? You took off your jacket and gave it to me. I didn't have to ask."

"Did I?" He shrugged, not really attending. "But how did we get the fire alight? Jack must've been home on leave, I suppose. Must've taken his tinderbox. I were lucky if I got away with *that* without him a-flaying me good and proper. Curious, ain't it? Remember all of it with you, clear as day, but I disremember what came after."

"I don't remember either. But, Jem, don't you see what I mean? I'll give you anything you want. You don't have to ask. Or, at least, you do, but only because I don't know how much you need."

He looked at me, eyes widening. "Oh. No. No, no, no. No, Master Willie, sir. That ain't...it's not...that ain't what I..."

"Will a pound do it, Jem?"

I blinked, suddenly cognisant of the most likely reason a man of Jem's type might ask me for money. He probably wanted to get married. My gut gave a very queer twist and a feeling almost of desolation swept through me. It was probably because once he had the money he would go.

"Or two pounds, perhaps?" I added. "And a new suit of clothes?"

"No, no, sir. It's very kind, but honest that ain't what I...I mean, there is something I wanted to ask of you, sir, begging your pardon, but that ain't it."

"It isn't?"

"No, sir."

"Oh. Then what, Jem? Would you like me to write you a letter of recommendation?"

"Er...well...perhaps if you would write it to yourself, sir."

"I don't quite..."

"Well, it's this, sir. I hope you'll beg pardon for my asking, but I was hoping as how you might be willing to take me on. I'll do *anything*, sir, that I will. And I hope as how the scrapes we got into as boys won't make you think I'm not a hard worker, for I have learned my lesson at sea and I am not a lad any longer, and I will work all the hours God sends and do anything you ask of me and that's a promise, sir. And it's true I don't know much of cows, sir, or pigs, but I know a little of sheep and of cabbages and potatoes, as you know, and of raspberries, for I learned that under Mr Scatcherd. And...and that is what I was wondering, sir, and why I came."

I blinked, so surprised my mind went blank. "I thought you wanted money. To get married, probably."

"No, sir." His expression was almost reproving. "Ain't the marrying type."

I said, "I was not looking to hire a man," because that was the truth.

"No, sir," he murmured, ducking his head and seeming to shrink.

"Midsummer Day is past," I added, because the quarter day would have been the time to take on new staff.

"So it is." His voice was very quiet.

"George does the garden and sees to the animals," I explained. "Mrs Fowke's brother."

"Aye. Course." His voice was a whisper. He was staring down at his boots. After a moment, he took a deep breath.

"Well, I am very sorry to have troubled you, Mr William, sir. And I thank you again for the meal, and it was right good to see you and I will be off."

His tone was all wrong. He was always polite, but he sounded formal, distant. He could have been any decent way-faring fellow, thanking me for a bit of charity.

"No—*no*," I blurted. "I mean, wait but a moment. Tell me, where will you go?"

"Don't rightly know, sir. Back to the...er...the tannery maybe, if they will have me."

I frowned. Things were going terribly wrong. "But you said you were not suited to the work."

"Well, maybe I can find something else." But there was something despairing in his tone.

"Wait, Jem. Wait. Where will you sleep tonight?"

"Don't trouble yourself over that, sir. I shall be all right."

"At least...no, Jem...I cannot let you go. At least you must stay one night."

"I could not put you to the trouble, sir."

"Jem, please. Will you not wait? Listen, I have had an idea."

"Aye, sir?"

"Yes. The thing is, George has not been well. He has terrible rheumatics. He can hardly walk sometimes. And he suffers from the ague too, very regularly. He is in bed with it now, I believe."

"Oh." He began to shake his head, very slow. "But I could not take a man's job from him, sir. I could not. Not if he were at death's door."

"No, no," I said, shocked. "Of course you will not be taking his job. But everybody knows he is old and that he suffers. So even though Midsummer's Day is past, people will perhaps understand that I am taking you on because of that. He needs help, do you see? There is too much for him to manage. So, it will not seem odd if I take you on as well. Will it?"

A sudden hope lit his face. "No, sir. I think people will understand."

"Do you? Yes, I think so too. Of course, it may seem profligate for a clergyman to have two men. Mr Hay who is the rector over the way in Medbridge has but one man and a boy, and Mr Chambers, who is vicar in Hockford, has but the one man, but that is because his boy grew too old and went for a soldier so he will certainly be getting another soon. And perhaps he will not even wait for Michaelmas? So that is perhaps all right. But the main thing, I think, is whether it would seem odd for the rector of Hunsford to have two men rather than one and a boy? Perhaps I must think on it."

"I did hear, sir, as how there was a Mr Melling, who was a parson in Hastings, who had two men. I knew one of them."

"Yes? And what did people say of Mr Melling?"

"He was a respected gentleman, sir."

"That is promising."

"Yes, sir."

"People did not say he was profligate?"

"I never heard so, sir."

I wished, as I had wished many times, that there existed a book that covered matters such as this and gave advice on which course of action would be approved by all. I could never tell which matters might be considered nothing much, and which might be considered beyond the pale.

Of course, the teachings of the church gave some guidance as to how most people might view some acts, but, alas, did not extend to such day-to-day practical matters as whether the rector of Hunsford might take on two men, given that one of them was often unwell.

In the past, I had sometimes used my folk as bellwethers. It was not that I took their advice, exactly, for they were uneducated people, but they were sensible and could at least provide reassurance.

"Jem, will you wait here for a moment? Promise you will not leave? Promise?"

"Aye, sir. I will wait."

"Do you promise me, though, Jem?"

"I promise."

I hurried into the house and tapped on the kitchen door, briefly noting, in my haste, that I had simply acted and not debated with myself. If only all of life could be so simple. "Mrs Fowke? Milly?"

Milly opened the door, Mrs Fowke at her shoulder, wiping her hands on a cloth. They were unrelated, of course, but I was struck afresh by their similarity. Not in looks, exactly, for where Milly was spare, Mrs Fowke was stout, yet they seemed cut from the same cloth. They did everything together and the hands of one seemed the hands of the other.

"Yes, sir?" There was enquiry in Milly's faded blue eyes.

"Ah, Milly. Yes. Mrs Fowke. I ah...I have been talking with Jem Binns. The...the fellow you have just been kind enough to give a meal. And...and I am of a mind to take him on." I paused but they continued looking at me steadily and did not speak nor give me any clue to their opinion, so perforce I must continue. "Yes. Because I have been worried about George for some time now. His health, you know, and the work being too much. Of course, George has his place here forever, as far as I am concerned, but Jem was my father's gardener's boy, so he knows a little of potatoes, you see. And he says he will stay. And he can do the heavier work and run my errands to Pettiford and so on, and George can show him what to do with the cows and how to make bread poultices for Pilot, and I think we should find ourselves well-situated. And there is a Mr Melling in Hastings who is a parson and has two men, although I am aware that Mr Hay and Mr Chambers have but one man apiece, although Mr Hay also has a boy. But I think, overall, that it is a good idea, probably. Although perhaps I must think on it some more."

My heart pounded as I waited for their response, and I realised, with something of a shock, that even if they confessed themselves amazed at my eccentric idea, I intended to ask Jem to stay anyway, for it was plain he wanted to and I ached to have him by my side once more.

Mrs Fowke said, "There, wasn't George saying only the other day as how he thought you might be thinking of taking on a boy or another man. Because of there being ever so much to do, sir, and him suffering terrible from his rheumatics as you know, sir."

Milly said, "You'll be wanting a bed made up for the lad, then, sir?"

From these remarks, I gathered they approved of the idea, or, at least, did not think it horribly unusual. Indeed, I rather thought that making up a bed meant the matter was settled and that Jem would be staying.

"Yes," I said. "A bed. Very good. Excellent. Yes, thank you, Milly."

"Is it all right, sir, if I put him in the little room that faces north?" Milly asked. "I would put him in with George, sir, only I don't think there is the space for another bed."

"Yes, yes, the little north room. That is quite all right."

"If I may, sir," Mrs Fowke put in, "If you are taking the lad on, he must have some new clothes first thing tomorrow and should sleep in the barn tonight for we don't want that jacket in the house, sir, begging your pardon, for it has more things living in it than a bit of old cheese, and we don't want to risk such in our nice new linen cupboards, that we don't!"

"Oh. No. We certainly don't. You are quite right, Mrs Fowke.

I remarked myself that his jacket was quite old and he will certainly need a new one. Yes, I will tell him he may sleep in the barn tonight and tomorrow I will take him to the village for new clothes."

I hastened back into the warm summer evening to tell Jem the good news, my heart so aflame with joy that all my apprehensions seemed, for a moment, as nothing.

# CHAPTER 4

I went to bed as usual that night but my heart was so full that I lay awake for hours. When events are unfolding, even events that most would consider joyous, I am usually too concerned with displaying the correct behaviour to take much enjoyment. Only afterwards, when I am alone and safe, can I cherish the memory.

The events of this evening were a jewel beyond price.

When I had told him he could stay, Jem thanked me a dozen times. That, I had expected. But before he had spoken a word of gratitude, he had looked me in the eye, properly. His shoulders had lowered and he had let out a great sigh. Then he had closed his eyes and stood there, as if his relief was so strong that he must let it overtake him. And it had felt to me as if we were boys and had narrowly escaped some terrible punishment. We were safe. We were together. For once, we had triumphed over the world.

After a while, I heard Mrs Fowke and Milly go up to the little room they shared beneath the eaves, and thereafter I heard them speaking together. I was in the best chamber at the front of the house and so too far away to hear what was said, but their voices came to me as a part of the natural world; leaves rustling in a breeze or water burbling in a brook. One of them laughed, and was hushed. The voices paused, then went on with the laughter still in them. I wondered what they could find to say to one another that they had not already said during the day. Perhaps they spoke of Jem.

I got out of bed and, going to the casement, eased it open. The nightingale was still singing in Butler's coppice and the air was cool and sweet. There was a near-full moon and I could make out every pale of the garden fence and the dark swags of the roses. I leaned out. To my left was the shed where we kept the gig and Pilot's tack, and there was the corner of the stable where Jem lay in the hay in his verminous jacket. Upstairs, the voices fell silent and did not resume.

Sometimes, as a boy, I had snuck out at night. I was not adventurous, finding the world quite dangerous enough without my needing to seek out more peril, and had I been caught I would certainly have been beaten. Perhaps it had been a desire to see the world in a different light, to see if I liked it better that way. Or perhaps I had simply wanted a story to tell Jem, for my moonlit excursions had occurred early on in our acquaintance when I had still believed I must impress him if I wanted him to remain my friend.

Not that my stories of midnight excursions would have been very exciting for I had generally gone no further than the garden or the churchyard. Only once had I gone as far as the yard of the Ship, where I had concealed myself behind some old barrels and spied upon the farmers and the fishermen going in and coming out. I had told myself one of them might drop a coin, but only because that sounded like the kind of thing I imagined an adventurous boy might say. Had anyone actually dropped a sixpence, I should have let it lie, as taking it would have been too much like stealing.

In any case, the fact was that observing people when I myself was unobserved had caused in me a particular kind of excitement. They could not mark what I did, nor discuss it, yet I was seeing some quintessence of their personalities, because they thought they were alone, and surely people were only truly themselves when they were alone. It was not that they did anything more untoward than breaking wind or making water in the alley, and likely they would have done those things anyway, whether they knew I watched them or not. But all the same, I had felt somehow rarified, both brave and safe, though not so safe I had dared to repeat the experience.

I turned from the casement, removed my nightshirt, and dressed. I was as silent as I knew how and had to remind myself several times that this was my house and I the master here. I could do as I liked. The stairs creaked so much I was sure Mrs Fowke and Milly would appear in their nightgowns and demand to know what was to do, but no one came.

I unbarred the front door and stepped out. The air was fresh, though the sun-warmed stone of the house was radiating heat. I took the path to the stables, towards the scent of hay and horse.

"Jem?" I whispered. "Jem."

He answered instantly. "Aye? Something amiss?"

Rustlings came from within and his head and shoulders appeared over the half-door.

"Nothing's wrong," I said. "I...merely wished to...to make sure you are warm enough and have everything you need. And now I have woken you."

"No, no, I was awake."

"Well, are you warm enough?"

"Yes, thank you, sir."

"Good, good. I'll go. You must be tired, having come all the way from Hastings." I turned away.

"Wait. A...a moment of your time, sir, if you please. Because I cannot sleep and that's the truth."

I turned back, pleased to continue my excursion a little longer. "Are you not tired, Jem?"

"I am that fagged, sir. I have walked a long way."

"I know. From Hastings, I think?"

"Well...that is what I wanted to tell you."

"Yes?"

"I...I didn't come from Hastings. Nor from Marshing, neither."

"Er...no? But you said—"

"I come from Sheerness."

I frowned in the dark. Sheerness was to the north-east, on the Thames, not far from Rochester and almost completely in the other direction. "What were you doing there, Jem? I thought you said the tannery was near Hastings?"

"I did, sir, but the fact is...well...I lied. I never was in no tannery. And I didn't ought to tell you an untruth. Because you have always been good to me and now I cannot sleep until I have set things right and told you the truth." He lowered his voice. "About my situation. And what I have done."

The shadows and the moonlight seemed suddenly sinister and my blood ran cold. "Your situation? Oh, Jem, what have you done?"

"Can I tell you my story first, sir? And then I hope you will understand and will let me stay."

"Tell me." My voice was harsh because I was afraid for both of us.

"I will sit down, if you don't mind, sir, for it is quite a tale. We could both sit on the bench outside."

I agreed to this and we sat side by side, our backs warmed by the sun that lingered still in the stable wall, though nothing could warm the chill that now clutched at my heart.

"You know I ran away to sea," he said.

"Yes, of course."

"Aye, well, it weren't no life. Was cruel hard and captain didn't like me and I never did get used to all that water. Missed the fields, see? And the woods. Even missed digging potatoes. Used to dream about grass beneath my feet."

"Could you not leave?"

He gave a mirthless laugh. "They know you for a tar, they

won't *let* you leave. I were pressed back in. More than once. Must have ships for the war, see?"

"Press-ganged," I breathed.

"Aye."

"But you got away in the end, obviously."

"Got a place on a merchant ship, sailing for the Caribbean. And when we got back to London I hid in the hold in the cotton bales, and they missed me. But they got me going over London Bridge a few hours later. All a-waiting they were, with their cudgels, a whole great gang of them. Weren't no escaping. They know a sailor when they see one because that's who they want. So, I said, 'no need to use that stick on me, mate. I'll come with you and willing, but let a man have a drink first, eh? Acos I just got back from the Azores and I want a pint'."

"And they let you go?"

"No, sir. They didn't trust me above half, but they let me buy them drinks and grub and I got a couple of bottles extra of hard grog, see? And they took us out to *The Ceres*, a guardship, what was lying off Sheerness, near the Nore, to hold us there afore they put us to work. And they put the other poor coves in the hold, but I said, 'no need for that, lads, come on let's have a drink'. And so we did, and after a while one of them gave me to understand that if I gave him everything I had, he might be able to give me something what I'd appreciate. He knew, see, what was in my head. Suppose he'd seen it a hundred times. So, I gave him what was left of my pay except what little I had hidden in my belt and he told me where to look when the time was right. And I'd been keeping an eye on the tide and so had he, certain sure, and when it was on the turn he gave me the nod. Them's treacherous waters off Sheppey Isle, see, and I had no wish to be swept out to sea. So, I looked where he said and found a bunch of pig's bladders, all blown up and tied together. And it was dark, so I made a rope fast and over the side I went."

I could not speak. I could almost smell the salt and the mud and hear the shift and creak of the ship. I could almost see the black waters slapping at the ship's side, cold and merciless, the currents racing this way and that.

"Jem. You could have been drowned."

"Aye. But I was damned if I—" He paused. "Beg pardon, sir. I have picked up some bad habits at sea. I mean, I could not stay."

"Yes, yes, I don't care about your language. Not when it is just us. But Jem...going into the sea. At night. And the currents."

"Ah, it were worse than I knew. Almost drowned. Not in the Thames but in the Medway. Treacherous, those currents be, but the tide swept me up at last to the north bank. And I got ashore, all covered in mud, and once I'd done coughing, I realised what a fool I was, for I was still dressed as a sailor, and the area all crawling with officers who would have liked nothing better than to haul me back."

"What did you do?"

"I walked. Couldn't risk going near Rochester, nor Gravesend, so I kept to the country lanes and rested in the woods when I couldn't walk no more, and drank from streams. And I went south and west and on the second day I met a cove who agreed to bring me some old clothes and some boots if I gave him the half-crown I had in my belt. Poacher, he was, I reckon. And he took my sailor's rig and gave me this hemmed pedicular jacket along with a pair of boots which don't fit and a heading for Sevenoaks, and here I am."

My heart was beating like a drum. He was hardly hidden, here in my stables. And while we had had no callers since he had arrived, all manner of people came to the rectory all the time. And I had not told my folk not to say anything about him. I had not known I ought to.

"But will anyone be after you? Will we get in trouble?"

He shook his head. "I ain't that important."

"Are you sure?"

"Certain sure." He glanced at me in the dark, and his tone was familiar, one boy to another. "Don't you worry, Master

Willie. Wouldn't have come if I'd thought it'd make trouble for you."

My breathing slowed. He had never lied to me about such things and indeed had more than once taken a beating upon himself to save me one.

"Well, that is all right then," I said.

"But I do need a place. And I cannot go to port towns, nor Marshing neither, for someone might recognise me and know me for a sailor. And I dursen't go back to sea, Master Willie. I can't. Would kill me to do so, I expect."

"Did you see battle, Jem?"

"Aye."

His voice was so low I could barely hear it. I wanted to ask him a hundred questions: where and when and which ships and under whose command and what it had been like, but something in his voice stopped me.

Instead, I said, "Will you tell me about it?"

He shook his head. "Begging your pardon, but I don't like to, see? Brings it all back. All I want is to forget it. I want to work in a garden again and live quiet. Should never have run away. Boy's dreams. Dangerous. Didn't know when I was well off. You know..."

He fell silent and I said, "Yes?"

"Do you remember—" he spoke as if dredging the words up from some very deep place, "—that place behind the raspberry canes in your Pa's old garden? In Marshing. Do you remember?"

"Yes."

"Ah. There was moss in the grass, and the hazel trees just there, weren't they, so the raspberries had some shade but could lift up their heads to the sun. Often went there, didn't we? Couldn't be seen from the house, there, nor from the road neither. Half-way secret, it was."

"I often remember it," I said. "I thought of it today because it was where we met. We ate raspberries there, from your hands."

"That we did. Well, I used to think of that place, at sea. I'd bring it all up, like, in my mind, and try to remember whether there was speedwell or self-heal at the edges, or both, and whether it was a thrush singing or a lark. And you was with me and it was safe, see, because you was keeping a lookout. And then I could go to sleep. Kept me going, that place. And I know I shall probably never see it again, but there are other places like it around these parts, I'll lay, if you will let me stay."

"Let you stay?" I frowned in the dark. "But it is already all decided, is it not?"

"Don't change nothing? What I have told you?"

"Of course not. Why should it?"

"You always did have your own opinion of the world, Master Willie."

I could hear the smile in his voice. I liked to hear it, but it worried me too, because there was something here I had not understood.

"Doesn't everyone?" I said.

"Well, aye, but you know what I mean. Always had your own way of seeing matters, different from the common view. Or you did. I did wonder, being as how you're a parson now and a man grown besides, that you might be different, but that was my mistake."

His words frightened me, for they made me realise a fresh danger with him in my household.

"No, no," I said, rather desperately, "Your mistake is otherwise. You must understand, I have a position to uphold. I am the rector of Hunsford. My opinions are not different or unusual. I comport myself always in a manner fitting for a rector. I am respectable and hold only those opinions that are fitting for a rector. Lady Catherine expects it. As do my parishioners."

There was a short pause, then he said, slowly and seriously, "I see. Of course. Beg pardon, Master Willie, sir. You are quite right and I was mistook."

"I do not see things differently from the common view," I said, desperate to make sure he understood.

"No, no. I beg your pardon. I would unsay that, if I could."

"I am the *rector*." It was essential to impress this point upon him. Essential.

"I understand. Certain sure."

There was some deep sympathy in his voice that blunted the edge of my fear. All the same, I added, "Jem, you must never say to anyone that I have unusual opinions or do or say anything unusual. Do you see? Not even to Milly or Mrs Fowke or George. Or anyone."

"Never give you away, I won't. Never. 'Tis all right. You mustn't worry."

"It's important. I have to be the rector."

"Aye. I know. I promise."

We sat for some moments in silence, for which I was very glad as I needed time to recover my equilibrium.

Presently, he said, "I can see a star. Moon's that bright I thought we wouldn't."

I looked up. "I can see several."

"That one—" he pointed, "—they call the harp."

"I always look for the hunter."

"Ah, we shall not see him tonight. Too early in the year."

"I know. But he's my favourite. Because of his dog. And the rabbit at his feet."

"Aye. Used to look for him at sea."

We sat a little longer in contemplation of the heavens and my mind began to thaw and I could think again.

"But, Jem, will you not explain why what you have told me should change anything?"

"Well," He spoke reluctantly, "Some folk would say I should go back and do my duty."

Now he had set it out, it was obvious, though it also seemed unreasonable that he should be asked to stay forever doing something so dangerous and so inimical to him.

"But you have done your duty for long enough, surely? You did it nine years or more."

"Aye, but some might name me a coward, sir. When we are fighting for our freedom because old Boney will not stop at home."

I could see this was a strong argument. What were the desires of one man, when set against the needs of a nation at war? What even the desires of two men? Because I certainly did not want him to go back to die in some blue Spanish sea.

My thoughts grew thick and slow again. Trafford would have helped me produce a stirring speech; something about how Jem should place his hope in the protection of Heaven and remember the pluck of our jolly Jack Tars, and so on, but for some reason I did not want to turn to Trafford with Jem. In fact, the idea was so distasteful, I shuddered.

"Cold, ain't you?" Jem said. "I'd give you this jacket but you don't want what comes along of it."

"I'm not cold. Listen, you have given nearly ten years to the navy. Surely you are due some time on land? If the French invade, we are but twenty miles from London, and they will doubtless overrun all Kent. We have already lost a lot of men hereabouts to the war. There are more than twenty widows in the parish and some of them have lost sons too. Though it is true not all of them are war widows. Mrs Watt's husband was kicked in the head by a horse, for example, and Mrs Lambard's died of a very violent stranguary, but her son died at Walcheren so she has very little, you know, having lost the farm. And there are three widows in the alms-houses who may not be relevant to my argument because they are very old and I don't know how their husbands died. But my point is that there are fewer men than there were. And you could join the local militia, if need be. They are all just local men, from Rosings and the village, and Mr D'Aubney drills them three times a week, though not at harvest time because then everyone is needed in the fields. Also, growing potatoes at the parsonage is important too." Speaking of the widows had reminded me. "Because people are hungry, even in times of war, or perhaps especially then. I am hoping to have plenty of potatoes this year so we may give a lot away."

"So, I may stay then?"

"Of course!"

He put a hand to his face and rubbed his eyes. His voice wavered. "Should have known you would not turn me away. You always were loyal. Always good to me. Always."

"I want you with me." My words were plain truth, but somehow they seemed to linger in the air, as if I had said something more meaningful than I knew.

"Aye." He cleared his throat. "Aye."

The stable wall had cooled and although I had said I was not cold a moment ago, I was growing cold now. Jem yawned suddenly and I found myself yawning too.

"I should go to bed," I said.

"Aye."

"I'm glad you have told me everything."

"Me and all."

I shifted forwards on the bench, but as I did so I turned to look at him and he spoke again.

"Strange, ain't it? Some lies rest easy in the heart. Don't matter, they don't, and I'd tell them again. Like telling the pressers I'd go with them. Don't feel like a lie, that don't, because them as who you're telling would do you harm if you told the truth. But some lies just rub and rub and won't give you no peace. I should have known I cannot lie to you. Anyway, I shall sleep now. Thank you, Master Willie. I shall do my best for you. Always."

"Good night, Jem," I said.

"Good night."

With that, I made my way back through the cool of the garden. I suppose I barred the door and that I was careful on the stairs. I must have undressed and put on my nightshirt, but the next thing I noticed was the pillow beneath my cheek and sleep overtook me.

# CHAPTER 5

It was well I slept deeply the night Jem arrived, because for the next three nights I tossed and turned as if the sheets were made of horsehair.

What if Lady Catherine thought me profligate to have taken on a second man? How angry would she be? What if she thought I should have hired a local man? What if she had had some deserving lad in mind for the position but had not yet informed me? What if I was forced to dismiss Jem? What if he hated me forever, or went back to sea and drowned?

The lack of sleep fuddled my memory and I forgot my little notebook at the alms-houses and my hat at old Mrs Meriweather's when I called on her with a bottle of Mrs Fowke's last year's elderberry cordial. And as for Jem, I could hardly bring myself to glance at him in case my joy somehow showed in a way it should not, though I could not help noticing how well he looked in the new brown breeches and jacket that we had got from the tailor. We had got him new boots as well, and he limped no longer.

On Thursday, I received a dinner invitation to Rosings.

I told Lady Catherine about Jem after dinner, over the cards. I had eaten almost nothing. I disliked most elaborate and highly flavoured dishes anyway, and tonight had been unable to choke much down, though I had, of course, been at pains to praise everything most highly.

She did not raise her eyes from the play, made a bid, and passed over the whole thing as if it scarcely mattered. I was limp with relief, afterwards, and lost every hand, to the silent vexation of Miss de Bourgh who was my partner.

That night I slept thirteen hours straight, even though I knew Lady Catherine might suddenly change her mind and find fault with me and my new man. All the same, as the days turned into weeks and she made no further mention of Jem and his place in my household, I began to think that perhaps, somehow, all would be well.

My own folk had no bad word to say of Jem, or, if they did, they did not share such opinions with me, although I gathered they found him rather shy and silent. George took him to the Oak Tree, when he was able, for a pot of ale and said he was a 'good willing lad, though don't know all there is to know about marrows'. Mrs Fowke remarked that he was very careful with his boots and not prone to spandling dirty footsteps on her nice clean floors. Moreover, she said he was never saucy, not even with Mr Butler's Tess, who came to milk the cows and who was so provoking. Milly put his tidy ways down to his once having been to sea in his younger days, from which I guessed that while Jem had not lied, he had been economical with the truth.

Jem himself was kept busy at a hundred jobs—clearing nettles and sow thistles from the garden beds, digging potatoes, trimming the sage and the thyme, mending a gate to stop the sheep getting in to strip the new plum trees, and dipping rags in coal-tar creosote to string around the garden edges to keep the Rosings deer at bay. Sometimes I would send him about the parish on errands: collecting new Geneva bands for me from the tailor, driving to Pettiford to collect some pipes of port, or taking some of our surplus beans to any family who I felt might be able to put them to good use.

My duties kept me busy about the parish during the day, for

I did much visiting of the old and the sick and infirm, but I took to finding Jem in the garden in the warm, still hour before supper. We would discuss how the peas were coming, or the marrows, and I would help him finish whatever job he was doing. We did not speak much then, except for brief, equable remarks about string or trowels or watering cans. Jem never spoke unless he had something to say, and the silences were easy.

I allowed myself, at such times, to imagine us both gardeners in the grounds of some large house like Rosings. We worked together always, side by side, and our lives were a succession of days with our hands in the earth and nobody expected me to make conversation or be gracious in society.

Jem, although he never seemed to hurry, was faster than me in all things, and could weed two rows of marrows to my one. Not that there was any whisper of competition between us. I disliked setting myself against my fellows because I craved always for companions, not rivals. Jem understood this and so we were at peace.

After supper I usually went into the garden again to enjoy the summer evening. Jem would be at one last job and checking all was well for the night. Sometimes he would show me something he had found: the nest of a willow warbler, a bright red and blue wasp, a Star of Bethlehem growing in the hedgerow. As the long evenings drew on, we took to lingering near the back paddock, leaning upon the gate and watching the cows as the sun went down.

At these times we often spoke of the past, of Marshing, and of the people we had known there. We fell into the way of playing what I suppose was a kind of game. I would say, "Could you still get from the parsonage to the old net-shed without being seen?" And he would ponder and say, "I'd go out near that old holly bush and into the churchyard. Go low through the gravestones and at the far corner was that hole in the yew. Remember? Through the hole and you be in Whiting's Lane.

Wait until all's clear. Along the lane past the saltings. Then cut across behind the boat sheds and there you are."

Or he might say to me "What if you were at that old barn and had to get home quick?" And I'd say "Well, if it was summer I'd go across the levels and past the pond with the willows; remember it? It was all right in summer, but any other time you'd be in mud above the knees. So, if it was winter I'd go north, through Brightling Wood. Then cross the road by Teal's Farm and go down that little track that came out near crossroads. You know, the one with the hazels where we found the dog that time. It was one of Mr Fleming's young hounds and we took it home and he gave us twopence. Remember? And then I'd run down the high street, cut through the yard at the Ship and be home."

My boyhood had not been happy and neither had his, for one of his elder brothers had been a bully, and after Jem's father had died, had seemed to find any excuse to find fault with Jem or to beat him. But somehow, recalling these hidden shortcuts and secret ways was both satisfying and pleasant. It was as if we were living our childhoods over, but this time without fear of punishment if we got home late or dirty.

My father had been considered a miser by his parishioners because he skimped on everything and paid nothing on time. He kept a lean table and had me wear his cast-offs. As a boy, my coats, which had been black when he had worn them, were all faded to rusty-charcoal or dark green. My breeches had ever been patched, and my linen sad and grey.

The truth was that my father had been terrified of running out of money. We lived in constant fear of the French, of course, and there seemed always to be some unexpected new tax or a hard winter or a failing bank. The living at Marshing was paltry and he had no family connections to count upon for his advancement. I learned, later, that he might have counted upon one Mr Bennet, who was some sort of distant cousin to me, and who had an estate worth two thousand a year, but my father had fallen out with that gentleman. The circumstances of the strife, he would never relate.

He was not illiterate, as I had heard it said, but he mumbled so terribly that some said he could not read his sermons. He did not send me to school until I was fifteen because he would not spare the money, but taught me at home, having me read from the Bible and other improving works.

He told me often that he had little hope of depending upon me in his old age, for he found me wanting in almost every regard and had no confidence in my ability to make my way in the world. He had died a few scant weeks before Lady Catherine had offered me the living at Hunsford. How I should have liked to give him the news that he should never have to worry about money again! But, alas, that joy had not been mine.

Usually, after we had spoken of Marshing, Jem would ask about my day, who I had seen and what they had said. I would get out my little notebook in which I had written the pertinent points, for I kept a record so I should not forget anything important such as the names of people's relations or my insights into the ways that a clergyman ought to behave. I would give him my news and we would talk of local events and doings. I valued these talks a great deal, for his remarks often gave me an interesting new perspective on matters.

Occasionally, at such times, he would let slip something about his life at sea. For example, that he had learned a bit of carpentry and so could mend the alms-house bench himself, or observations about human behaviour, such as that occasionally in life two people simply cannot get on, and will find any reason to find fault with one another, such as he had seen with two midshipmen of his acquaintance.

I made it clear to him early on that he must attend church on Sundays because I did not believe it would be thought fitting for members of my household to neglect that duty. I was nervous the first few times, for he had never seen my Sunday performance as rector before and I was worried he might find me wanting, even though I knew he would say nothing.

Some people, I am told, find churches to be places of peace and succour. I had ever found them steeped in anxiety, for as a child I had often been punished for looking bored or not appearing to attend to the service, though in fact I had listened to every word. Now, of course, I must perform said service for persons who were judging me and likely finding me dull.

The parish church at Hunsford was therefore, for me, a place of tension, besides being rather cold and damp even in the summertime. The interior was plain white plaster, Lady Catherine's ancestors having had no truck with popery. Also, I had, on my induction, employed a man to scrape the mould from the walls of the chancel and to cover it in fresh whitewash. The church's sole adornment was a pair of tablets with the Ten Commandments inscribed upon them, which hung on the eastern wall.

The bareness made me feel very exposed when I mounted the three-decker pulpit, there being but little to distract the attention of the flock away from me. Of course, that was the point, but nonetheless I often wished the church boasted some decorative stained glass or a carved rood screen as I had seen in other churches during my curacies in Sussex and in London.

However, after the first few services, with Jem making no remarks afterwards about my performances and treating me no differently than before, I more or less forgot he was there and concentrated simply on reading the services, and my sermons, as loudly as I could, as usual.

One sweltering evening in August, Jem said he had something to show me. There was an eagerness to his manner that led me to the conjecture that it was something special. It had been a long hot day and I felt I had said the wrong thing to Mr Butler when I had met him in the lane as he had been quite curt with me. I was tired and cross with myself and therefore with everything. I was disinclined to linger in the heat, even with Jem, but I could not disappoint him.

He led me out of the garden and into the back paddock, round the back of the barn and across to the snicket gate set into what George called a carvet, being a hedgerow of some age and thickness. The gate was not much used as it led nowhere but the wilderness; a thicket that sloped down to various sedges and willows that grew about a small brook. Some of my ill temper fell away. We had seen a peregrine of late, perhaps Jem had found its nest?

"Where are we going?" I asked.

Jem glanced over his shoulder and smiled. "Not far."

He led me unerringly into the wilderness, through some sweet chestnuts, around a hawthorn, under a curtain of ivy and down, towards the brook. As I scrambled after him, I noticed, here and there, freshly cut branches which told me he had cleared a path. All the same, we must pick our way, and the exertion and the closeness of the trees caused my head to pound and the sweat to pour down my face and my back.

A musical trickling drifted towards us. A gleam came through the trees, the sound of water grew louder and we found ourselves on the edge of the brook. It was narrow at this point and had no name that I knew, though it was a tributary of the Gadway, since it curved, eventually, around the far side of my western pasture and thence beneath a low bridge in the road. It meandered through Butler's coppice to join the Gadway proper, which flowed through Hunsford.

At the brook, Jem turned left and continued picking his way through brambles and ferns. If we walked far enough, we should get to Rosings Park. I said as much.

"Ain't going that far. Fact, we're nearly there." He paused and turned to me. "Close your eyes."

"But why?"

"You'll see."

I greatly disliked surprises. I preferred the earliest apprehension of facts so I had time to consider them and decide upon the most appropriate response. But Jem was smiling and holding out his hand. I would not have done it for anyone else in the world, but for him I closed my eyes and reached.

His hand was huge and hot and hard as horn. My own lay damp within it so it felt we were joined by a melting ball of wax. The sensation was such that I wanted both to pull away and to have him hold me like that forever, but he led me but half a dozen paces and let go, saying, "Now just you take a glim at thissen."

A slender pool lay at our feet, four or five yards across at the widest point and perhaps half as deep. A huge old willow grew upstream and in narrowing to flow around this giant, the water had carved out this trough for itself before flowing on. All was in shade but for a dappling of gold and a single ray of sunlight which passed through the willow's branches and pierced the water like a coppery sword.

"Why, it's beautiful." My voice was hushed for this felt a secret place. "I never knew there was a pool here."

"Don't nobody know, excepting a fox and a little old urchin. Saw a deer once."

The water flowed with barely a murmur, its movement betrayed only by dimples and swirls, and the occasional submerged leaf gliding by. Sweat dripped down my forehead and I wiped it with my handkerchief. I longed to take off my shoes and stockings and bathe my hot feet.

"Could we sit down, do you think?" I said.

"Your land. Reckon we may do as we please."

I found a fallen tree that lay a few feet back from the poolside and perched upon it. Jem threw himself down into the undergrowth, grinning at me from its depths, fern fronds dancing about his face. Above us, the sky was a lattice of gold and green and blue.

"'Spikenard and saffron; calamus and cinnamon, with all trees of frankincense'," I said. "And a 'well of living waters' too."

"Living waters, aye."

"Song of Solomon. Four fourteen. And a bit of four fifteen."

"Aye. Ain't twigged yet, have you?"

"Haven't...what?"

"Why I brung you here."

"You wanted to show me the pool."

"Aye." He waved a dismissive hand. "Guess again."

"You...something about irrigation for the garden? We could dig channels. I don't know though, Jem. It's quite low-lying. We'd need a pump."

"Go on with you!" He gave a short laugh. "Brought you here to bathe."

"Bathe?" I felt my eyes grow round. The pool was large enough, just about, but surely a score of farmers' wives and their daughters could be thronging the thicket even now. I glanced about. Of course, there was no one. Just the trees. "I can't bathe."

"Why not?" Jem asked. "Always used in summertime."

"We were children. Boys."

He looked at me steadily. "Ain't deep. Won't drown."

"It's not that. I'm the *rector*."

"Parsons don't bathe?" He lifted his eyebrows in obvious disbelief.

"Someone might see."

"Who?" He looked around, making it clear there was no one. "Excepting maybe old Master Tod."

"You mean the fox?"

"Aye, the fox. And he don't tell no tales, the rascal."

"I...I just can't."

Something made small ripples on the surface of the pond. There must be fish. Sticklebacks, perhaps. I craned forwards.

Maybe it was newts. At the far side of the pond, the water grew deeper, the colour of ale. The water would be refreshing, but not icy. I could wash away all the sweat and stink and strain of the day. And afterwards, when I had dressed, my skin would feel cool, as if it carried within it the memory of the water.

"Maybe you ain't rector down here." Jem had put his arm over his face. "Not in this little old wilderness where no one ever comes. Down here, maybe you're just plain Master Willie as was?"

I stared, glad he wasn't looking at me, for his words were causing strange feelings to course through me, as though the current of the stream had risen up and was washing something away.

It would be like calling on Trafford, only the other way around, because this time, I would be calling on myself. Or, myself as I once had been: Master Willie: Young, hungry, lonely, solemn, terrified of doing the wrong thing. And yet, somehow, also able to splash about with Jem in the eel pond at Branley Chase on hot summer afternoons.

"I don't know," I said.

He began to smile. "Know you want to."

"What if someone comes? Mrs Fowke, or Milly."

"They don't come down here." He lifted his arm, glanced at me. "I'll keep watch though, if you like. Downstream."

"Maybe I could bathe my feet." That was something even Trafford might do since it was true there were no ladies about, nor likely to be any.

"Aye. Ease into it, like."

I removed my shoes and stockings and bathed my feet, and presently Jem said he was just going downstream a little way and pointed out a branch that grew at a good angle for hanging my clothes over. But as he turned away, I was seized with sudden fear, almost panic. It was not of being left alone, exactly, for it was a beautiful place and on my own glebe land. I had a right to be here. I could not explain why my heart pounded, nor why his leaving should feel so unacceptable.

"Jem?"

He half-turned, eyebrows raised.

"Don't go."

"Will I not keep watch?"

"No. You should bathe too." I had not known that was the reason until I said it, but of course that was what was wrong with him leaving. In the past we had always bathed together. "You want to, don't you?"

"Well." He looked at me, head cocked to the side. "Won't deny I'm all of a muck sweat."

"I'll go in if you will."

He smiled, for it was what I always used to say, and said, "Aye, all right then."

He began to unbutton his waistcoat and I did the same with clumsy fingers. I removed my neck-cloth and paused, but Jem was pulling his shirt over his head and unlacing his boots. I did not want to get left behind so I began to hurry as well, and soon I was undressing as if the woods were on fire and my life depended upon getting into the water as quickly as possible.

It felt strange to stand naked in the woods and I could not help glancing over my shoulder, still half expecting to see Lady Catherine herself marching down the slope with horrified disapproval writ across her face.

But Jem was already stepping gingerly into the brook, and wading to the deepest part. His bulk was white in the dappled shade, only his hands and face burnt nut-brown by the sun. He knelt, then plunged forwards, submerging briefly. He rose with a dog-like shake of the head, then crouched there, only his head and shoulders above the level of the water, hair shining with wet.

"Cold!" He was puffing and grinning. "Good though. Deeper than it looks."

I followed his path into the water, first wading, then kneeling, then allowing myself to fall forwards into the water. He had stirred up debris from the bottom and old leaves and twigs brushed my face and the sudden cold made my nerves shout and quiver. I surfaced, gasping and spluttering, and he clasped my wrist and pulled me to the head of the pool where there were willow roots to cling onto.

"There." He shook his head again to get the wet hair out of his eyes. "Prime, eh?"

"Yes. Prime."

I let myself stretch out the length of the pool next to him. Above us, midges danced, and the smell of green things and flowers and leaf mould was everywhere, as if all the perfumes of the year from spring to winter were distilled into the brook. As it flowed, the water caressed me in places I did not often think of; the small of my back, my fundament, the tops of my thighs.

Beside me, he turned, and let his face rest under the water for a moment. He lifted it, opened his eyes. "Ho, that's good! That'll wash away the heat."

"Yes."

"Glad you got in now, ain't you?"

I nodded.

"You always hemmed and hawed and you was always glad. Remember?"

"I suppose I did."

"Not as big as that old eel pond though, is it?"

"This is better. It's *ours*."

He smiled. "Yours."

"You found it."

"Ours, then," he conceded, for it had always been our fancy as boys that discovery led to some private understanding of ownership, though only between the two of us, for we had known well that nothing was truly ours.

Presently, in some silent accord, we left the water. I put on my still-warm shirt and drawers and breeches and we sat at the side of the pond to let ourselves dry. My skin felt smooth and clean and the air so warm it was a caress upon my brow and my bare calves and feet.

I felt languid, but at the same time as if I could walk twenty miles and still have heart for twenty more. It was a sensation I had not experienced for many years. In fact, the last time I had felt this way had also been with Jem.

"I missed you," I said, "When I came home from school and you were gone."

"Aye. Sorry. Missed you too."

"Couldn't you have waited? To say goodbye?"

"Don't know as how I could."

"Oh." I picked at my stockings, crestfallen.

It had been such an awful homecoming. I had paid my respects to my father and acquitted myself as best I could at the interview that followed, in which his unhappiness at how much money I had spent had featured greatly, though I had paid only for those services that had been absolutely necessary and I had tried to assure him of that fact.

Once he had dismissed me, I had run out of the house to find Jem, and the gardener had told me, with a shrug, that the poor fellow had run away to sea. I had been so bereft that I had felt that Jem had died. Or perhaps that *I* had. I had wept for days.

"It were like this," he said, and then fell silent for so long I thought he had decided not to speak further. The dead leaves in the pool that had been stirred up by our bathing gradually sank or were carried away by the current. He said, "Look, you were gone off to school. And I thought you'd come back and...and... realise. And I couldn't have that. So, I thought, you'd gone off to be a man so I should do the same. So, I went. And that's how it was."

"But, Jem, what should I realise?"

He glanced at me and looked down. "About me."

"I don't..."

"You're *gentry*. Your Pa was the parson. And me..." he gave a short laugh. "I were nothing. Gardener's boy. No prospects.

Didn't know my letters. Still don't. Ain't brave. Face all anyhow." He touched his lip.

"I like your face." I frowned, thinking of a hundred times he had shown courage when we were boys. I had seen him wading in to break up dog fights and calming frightened horses and all manner of other feats. He had not even been afraid of the gander who had belonged to the landlord at the Ship. "How can you say you're not brave?"

He shook his head, as if to dismiss my words. "I thought things would change when you got back. Thought you'd have learned not to want to go about with the likes of me. And if you didn't learn it at school, I thought you'd learn it at university, or after you took orders."

I shook my head. "I learned the opposite. I learned I like no one so well as I like you."

"Ah." He glanced at me again. "You know, at sea, I saw some wonders. Fish what could fly and sharks with swords on their noses, but that there beats those things hollow. Still don't understand it."

"But we're friends," I protested, for I did not like his line of thinking. "It was one of the first things you said to me. Don't you remember?"

"Don't know as I do, but since you say it I know it must be true."

"Yes, it is true." I paused. "Can I tell you a story? About my time at Oxford?"

"Course."

"I read Classics. You know, Latin and Greek. I had a tutor. Everyone does. One goes to his rooms and one talks and answers questions and so on. Anyway, in my first year, I saw my tutor with two other men: Bailey and Ashford. Bailey, I think, did not like me. He seldom addressed me if he did not have to, but Ashford was very amiable. He smiled a lot and would often walk with me afterwards, for our rooms lay in the same part of the college. And as we walked, he would tell me things, about his sister getting married and his father losing money when his bank failed, and his cousin taking ill. I never had much news of my own to impart, but I listened and responded in a manner which I felt was appropriate; asking pertinent questions, and making relevant remarks."

"Aye."

"Then in my second year, things changed, and I no longer saw Ashford in my tutor's rooms. And I was sorry, because I missed him and I used to wonder how his sister was getting on in her new home, and whether his cousin had recovered, and so on." I fell silent, lost in the memory.

"Some friends do fall by the wayside," Jem remarked. "Pity, that."

"No, no, that is not the end of my story. The thing is, near the end of my second year, I met him again. I had seen him about, in halls, but we had not spoken, then we ran into one another. He had been visiting a man in a room near mine and we met at my door just as I was going out. And I greeted him and asked after his sister and he looked so startled that I felt duty bound to remind him that we had shared a tutor the previous year. And he looked blank, and then his face lit up and I was happy for I could see he remembered me after all, and then he said 'Ah, yes, Wilson, isn't it?' He couldn't remember my name, you see. Not that I should have held that against him, for a man may easily fail to recollect such minor details, but it soon became clear he didn't really remember me at all. He asked after my mother, for example, and of course she'd been dead for nearly twenty years, and I know I had told him that.

"Anyway, he went his way and I went mine and we never spoke again. But the thing was...I had thought—" my voice wavered and I cleared my throat to hide it, "—I had thought we were...well, not good friends, but at least friendly acquaintances. I remembered everything about him; all the details of his sister's preferences in gloves, and the names of his father's hounds, and...and everything. But he had not thought of me as a friend.

Indeed, it was plain he had not thought of me at all. If he recalled me in any way, I was simply that fellow with whom he had once shared a tutor. Nothing more. Our talks had meant nothing to him. And I...I own that it hurt me. Because I made no other acquaintance at university, but I thought I had made one, and then it turned out I had not even made that."

"Ah." His voice was soft. "Cruel hard, that was."

"I have no gift for friendship," I said. "I wish I did, and I do my best, but somehow it does not happen. Except with you. Somehow, with you, it has always been easy. And I know our stations in life are different, but that has never mattered to me. Not in private."

"Well, then." His voice low. "Don't matter to you, it don't matter to me."

I was content with that, though I felt raw at having told him my Ashford story, for the memory of my last encounter with the man ever set me writhing internally with humiliation. My hope that I had made a friend felt pathetic, even to me.

We sat a little longer and then Jem arose and I followed him out of the wilderness and back into the real world with all its bafflements and cruelties, but that night, in bed, the memory of the water, and of Jem, refreshed my limbs and my heart and I slept.

# CHAPTER 6

One evening in late September we again went down to bathe.

By now, we had bathed twenty-seven times.

After the second time, Jem had vouchsafed to me that he had been obliged to tell George and Milly and Mrs Fowkes where we had been, for they had been curious about our absence from the garden. He had felt, quite rightly, that it was better to tell as much of the truth as he could. So, he had told them I had taken a fancy to bathe in a pool in the brook because of the heat, but that I did not want it getting about in case Lady Catherine thought such behaviour indelicate in a clergyman.

He told them I had taken him along to keep watch and that he did not mind for he could sit at his ease in the shade and had besides enjoyed plunging his head into the pool. He said Mrs Fowke had tutted rather and hoped I should not catch cold, but with their curiosity assuaged they never again questioned our brief absences.

Every time we reached the pool, I looked for the sticklebacks, and the ferns which grew in the cool place beneath the fallen tree, and for the sword of sunlight piercing the water. Then, once we were in the water, we would lounge at the head of the pool, where, above us, hung always a velvety brown spider in her place in the centre of her web. I do not much care for spiders usually, and had she lived anywhere in the rectory I should have instructed Milly to remove her forthwith. But down by the pool, I liked to see her because she was a part of it all and belonged there. I looked for her as one might look for a friend.

The first few times I had not stayed in the water long, and had hastened to dress afterwards. Not because I truly believed any ladies would venture down the rough path to take fright at my nakedness, but more because the place felt too new and therefore I did not quite trust yet in its beauty nor its sanctity from prying eyes.

After our twenty-eighth bathe, the place felt as safe as my own bed chamber. I pulled my shirt on over my head and that was sufficient for decency. That familiar pleasant lassitude was coursing through my veins and I lay back in the ferns, caring for nothing but the gentle shift of the warm air on my limbs. Jem lay down too, separated from me by a few green fronds. Above us, sunlight shimmered through the treetops. If I moved my head a fraction of an inch, a shaft of light all the colours of the rainbow seemed to shoot down to my eye. If I moved my head back, it vanished. I thought, *this is happiness.*

I turned my head and Jem was watching me through the ferns.

"What?" I said, for there was a look in his eyes that made my belly clench.

"No one about," he remarked.

It was the sort of comment I tried not to make, for it was very obvious, and therefore needless. However, I thought it a nice reassurance.

"No one," I agreed. "We're quite alone."

"No one ever comes. Not ever."

"True," I said, happily, for it felt good to revel in the fact of our solitude.

"Remember..." He stopped.

"Remember what?"

He sighed, not in frustration, I did not think, but more as if he was making his mind up to something. "Something we used to do. A few times. Afore you went to school."

"Bathing, you mean?" I furrowed my brow in bewilderment.

He shook his head. "Not that. Something else. Something I showed you. Remember? It were private. You liked to watch it."

"Oh!" A prickle of excitement ran through my nerves. "You mean—" We were not speaking loudly, but I lowered my voice to a whisper, "—frigging?"

He had taught me the word, which he had learned from his brother. Apparently, all men did it. Sometimes, they did it together.

"Aye. That," he said.

"Yes, I remember." I could hardly catch my breath.

"Aye. Well. Want to watch me now? Like we used?"

We had done it perhaps half a dozen times in the past, but it had not crossed my mind that such things were still a possibility between us.

"Not if you—" he began.

"Yes," I said, quickly. "I want to."

He grinned, shut his eyes, and turned his head away. That was for me, to give me privacy, and I caught my breath against a sudden surge of tenderness, because he had remembered all this time that while I liked to watch him, I did not like him watching me.

Through the ferns, his right hand was sliding low, down to his privy parts, which he rubbed through the fabric of his shirt. The cloth was damp and a blush of pink showed through. His member grew hard and lengthened and he ran his fingers along it as it lay enshrouded. That mere glimpse of his flesh through the weave of his shirt made my own privy parts tighten so fast my head seemed to spin.

He stood his member up from the base so the damp cloth was raised like a tent. The tip of his member was blunt and wet and his shirt became quite transparent over it. I put a hand to my own member, which was pulsing to attention. The fern fronds bowed in a slight breeze and momentarily obstructed my view of him. I shifted, craning my neck to see better. The breeze slackened and I had to shift again.

My breathing was coarse in my ears. I told myself he did not know I was watching, and that I was seeing something I ought not to see. Of course, it was not true, but the thought that it could be true inflamed me. My member throbbed.

He lifted his right hand to his mouth, spat on it, and flicked his shirt up with his other hand, pulling it above his chest. His member rose red over his white belly, and I stuffed my free fist into my mouth to stifle the mewling sound I wished to make. I must be silent. I must not give myself away.

He brought his wet hand down and took his member within it. He made a sound, barely a murmur above the music of the stream, but my balls were tightening and I should not last. I never did.

Part of me wanted to reach over and touch him, but in the past he had not permitted that and in any case, it would ruin the illusion that he did not know I was there. Instead, I squeezed and pulled at my own member, until he gave a groan and gouts of white matter shot forth from his member onto his stomach and chest.

I turned on my side, angling my member towards the ground to keep my shirt clean. Four pulls, five, and I was no longer myself. I was a hot and sweaty hand and the fire of an erect cock. I was the sunlight pulsing through the treetops, the current of the stream. And then I was spending and knew nothing, except that Jem was with me somewhere and we were safe.

Afterwards, I opened my eyes and there was a small spatter of white on the ground before me, already sinking into moss. I covered myself with my shirt and lay back, eyes closed, too drained to do anything but admire the patterns of red and black that seemed to shift and fade on the insides of my eyelids.

After a few moments, Jem said, "All right?"

"Yes."

"Ah. Good."

Presently, he arose and went to the brook to rinse himself off. I sat up, then we dressed, as usual, without comment, and made our way up out of our beloved wilderness to our other lives.

I went into the house, for it was a Thursday, and on Thursday evenings, I usually sat at my desk to study the lesson for Sunday and to go through my books of sermons to decide which I could best adapt. My method, of which I was quite proud, was to select a suitable sermon and then to rewrite it, sentence by sentence, in alternative words. In this way I could be sure of expressing no unfitting idea or sentiment by mistake, while still offering some novelty of approach to anyone in my flock who may already be familiar with the sermons in that particular book.

Today I took up a book at random, drifted to my easy chair and sat gazing out the open windows. Late summer gazed back at me, scented with honeysuckle and ringing with the chirrups of small birds.

A most extraordinary peace settled over me. All was well. All had ever been well, and always would be. The feeling was so remarkable that I tested it by recalling some embarrassments of the past; occasions when I had said the wrong thing, or been unable to say anything at all. Amazingly, my tranquillity did not waver. Indeed, at that moment, upsetting myself over such mistakes seemed ludicrous because it did not help me improve. If anything, the more I upset myself, the more self-conscious I became, and the more self-conscious I became, the more mistakes I made. So, I should never again berate myself for making mistakes. I should do my best not to repeat them, but not make myself miserable for being imperfect.

It was Jem, of course, who had made me feel this way, and yet if anyone had seen us earlier down by the brook, they would say I should send him away and spend the rest of my life repenting.

Outside, the hollyhocks rustled, blooms tossed by the

breeze. I closed my eyes, nestled my head more comfortably against the wing of the chair and let my mind drift. For some reason, I was taken back to the shadowy place beneath the dining table in my father's house in Marshing. I could see the dark lustre of the table's legs, surrounded by the forest of slender chair-legs.

I was nine years old and a woman was sobbing in the hall. It was Miss Hindmarsh, an old maid of forty, with red hands and a wart on the side of her nose. I did not know her well, though she was kind and had once helped me by mending a rent in my breeches because she had noticed it when I was passing by her cottage. She had lived there, until yesterday, with her brother Thomas, who, being prone to melancholy, had cast himself the previous day from the top of a cliff. I hugged my knees.

My father was refusing to allow Thomas Hindmarsh to be buried in the churchyard. Miss Hindmarsh was begging otherwise. If I looked sideways, there was the hem of Miss Hindmarsh's worn coat, trembling before my father's equally worn shoes and stockings. I stared at a table leg instead, at the nicks and dents. My father was recounting, with some indignation, the testimonies of George Decks and Mary Haight, a courting couple who had been lying in a meadow not twenty yards from the cliff edge when Thomas Hindmarsh had approached. George Decks had risen to his knees and yelled at the man to beware. Thomas Hindmarsh had glanced at him, once, and run over the edge. Suicide, plain as day. Therefore, he could not be buried in the churchyard.

Miss Hindmarsh gasped between sobs, as if she too were running towards a cliff edge, or perhaps away from one. The sound hurt my ears. The indignation in my father's voice had an edge that was equally painful, and, looming above all were the thoughts I was trying not to think: the gaping horror of George Decks and Mary Haight; the hopeless suffering of Thomas Hindmarsh and the terror he must have felt at the top of his long fall.

A body must be buried, lest it stink. Also, bereaved people sometimes needed a grave to visit because they missed the person so violently that they needed somewhere to go, something to do, like taking flowers to the grave. Had I not myself sometimes visited the grave of my mother when I had been so unhappy I had not known what else to do with myself? But such visits made no difference to the dead; they were simply a way for the person left behind to express grief.

The difference between the consecrated ground within the churchyard and the un-consecrated ground without seemed nothing to me. The difference was that some distant priest—a man not unlike my father—had said some words over the churchyard. The words of priests were supposed to matter because they were a conduit for God. That much I knew. But I had always thought God to be one of those elaborate games of make-believe by which my elders set so much stock. One must say one believed, for that was what decent people said, but surely, I had thought, none of them really thought it was true. To me, religion was a charade, something akin to the polite lie that ladies of a certain class lacked bodily functions, or the fiction that the poor had nothing because they were lazy.

I was certain my father was no conduit for any unearthly power. I had never seen any proof and I had lived with him forever. So, the ground was the same, whether within or without the churchyard. That meant that both my father and Miss Hindmarsh were upsetting themselves for something imaginary. How could they not see how ridiculous they were?

I was glad of the table above me, strong and certain, for the world felt a dangerous place when my elders could not be trusted to use the evidence of their eyes and ears to arrange matters.

Occasionally, the lessons my father read on a Sunday seemed sensible. Thou shalt not kill, for example, seemed logical, for one did not want to live in a world in which people killed each other. But then English soldiers killed the French and my father encouraged the congregation to rejoice. What good was a philosophy in which opposing truths were both true?

My father had opened the front door and all but pushed Miss Hindmarsh out through it. He had said his piece and would hear no further argument. He shut the door. She stayed there in the porch for a time, weeping, until presently she ceased and went away. But I stayed beneath the table all the afternoon, hiding from a world which seemed suddenly even more cruel and unreasoning than I had supposed.

When I was sixteen and my father fell ill, I had tried most heartily to find some meaning and comfort in prayer and the church. I knew I must be a clergyman because my father would consider no other course for me, and in truth I did not argue because at least I knew what was expected of a clergyman, having watched my father and spent so much time at church. I knew my catechism and my articles. But no matter how I tried, my prayers were empty and the services raised no more sentiment in me than the ritual of my morning toilette.

I had thought, for years, that this lack of religious feeling meant I was in some way broken, or at best, incomplete. But the snicket gate through the carvet, the sight of Jem's back as he preceded me down the path, the brook and the trees and the spider and watching Jem through the ferns...yes, all that made me feel something.

Indeed, for the first time in my life, I knew what men meant when they spoke of the divine.

Three days later, we went to bathe again. Afterwards, as we lay in the ferns, Jem again asked me if I would like to watch him. I said that I would, and matters progressed in the same way as they had done previously. But as we lay there afterwards, I allowed myself to sink into so delightfully torpid a state that my body betrayed me and I broke wind, loudly.

I had ruined our perfect idyll. I stammered an apology, and something about too much of Mrs Fowke's rhubarb fool.

Jem gave a short laugh and said, dismissively, "Heard worse at sea."

"All the same," I said, still mortified.

"No, no," he added, "It's a sad arse as can't sing sometimes, ain't it?"

I looked at him through the ferns. His eyes were shut, his mouth softened by a smile. Everything in his demeanour told me that he really did not mind and that I had spoiled nothing.

Of course, I did not wish to start conducting myself regularly in a coarse or vulgar manner, but I had often felt, in refined company, that my very corporeality was something of which I ought to be ashamed. I should not sweat, nor cough, nor hiccup, nor allow myself any of the other natural functions to which the body cleaves. That Jem was not disgusted by me was such a relief that my heart filled with the most extraordinary feelings of tenderness and gratitude and, oddly, not a little admiration. He, and he alone, allowed me to be the poor forked animal that I was, and did not judge me for it.

I was still staring at him when he remarked, "That was prime, before, eh? I like it; knowing you're watching."

I mumbled something about liking it too.

"Wasn't sure you'd still want to do such as yon," he added.

"Why not?"

"Well, you being the parson now." He grinned, suddenly. "A parson would never say 'why not?'."

"Mr Collins would never say it," I agreed. "But down here I am not him. Remember?"

"Aye, I remember." He paused. "Don't you get weary? Always playing a part?"

"Weary?" I was often so tired I felt I could not live through another day. "Yes. But I have no choice."

"But you're a gentleman. Surely..."

"I had to become a clergyman. Father insisted. You know that. And in any case, I should never have made a soldier, should I? And I have no head for business. So, I did not disagree. And I suppose I am a bad clergyman as most men would judge it, for I have no calling, but I do my best to speak and behave as the rector to everyone but you. I must live my life somehow, but I do not understand the world, nor the way other people think. I do not really understand why they find some behaviours offensive and others delightful, and I don't suppose I ever shall. I am different, I think, in many ways. You have said so yourself. And I cannot help that. So, I hide in plain sight to all but to you. For if anyone discovered my true nature, I do not know what they would do to me."

I could feel his gaze upon me. "They like you, you know. Folk here."

I was startled into looking back at him. "They *like* me? Mrs Fowke, you mean? Milly and George?"

"Aye, them. You ain't troublesome and you ain't turned George off when another man might. Appreciate that, he do. And you always call her 'Missus'. Polite, see? Won't hear a word against you, she won't. True gentleman, she says you are. But I don't mean just them. Mean others, too, hereabouts." He paused. "Can't speak for the gentry, mind. But the common folk."

"They like me? *Why*?"

"Well..." He lay back in the ferns and began ticking points off on his fingers. "You ain't always off shooting or bull baiting like young Mr Chambers over Hockford way. Squarson, they call him, and not friendly-like neither. Wishes he was the squire, don't he? You don't. You act like a parson. You show an interest and do your duty and you're free with your charity. Penny here, sixpence there, eggs to widows and that. You gave young Betsy Milner a pound towards burying her Ma in Norwich. Great talker is young Betsy. Told everyone. And you tip when you should and pay your bills on time."

I blinked. "Any parson would do those things."

He shrugged. "Your Pa didn't. Mr Chambers don't. Nor did the last rector who was here afore you, by all accounts. Couldn't keep his hands to hisself neither." He shook his head. "Didn't dare touch Mrs Fowke, but Milly had a terrible time, poor old girl. Couldn't be alone in a room with him but he was trying something on. You ain't like that." He glanced at me. "Won't hear that sort of thing from Lady Catherine." He shrugged. "But then I'll lay she didn't know."

"No. She cannot have known," I said faintly.

In fact, Lady Catherine had spoken often of the rector before me, and always in the most glowing terms. I remembered how Milly had been when I had first arrived at Easter-time; pinched and nervous. Indeed, I had thought maybe she was sickening for something, or perhaps was grieved by the death of the previous incumbent. Also, while I had not marked it at the time, now I thought of it, it was true that she had seemed to avoid being alone with me. She did not do so now.

"Oh, and you give powerful complicated sermons," Jem said.

"And that's a good thing?"

He shrugged. "Oh aye. I mean, there's some as likes more blood and thunder, but they know Lady Catherine don't hold with that methodist kind of carrying on, and anyway, there's plenty as likes your style—all them long words and that. Proper, ain't it? And you always keep it to twenty minutes. There's plenty as appreciate that."

"I am doing my best," I said, allowing myself to bask in this unexpected feeling of having done the right thing, it having never occurred to me that my parishioners thought well of me. Generally, I assumed they were disappointed in me, irritated by me, or, at best, that they did not think of me at all.

"I know." He nodded, in a considering manner, then fell silent.

We lay like that for a while but my unease began to grow, for in the past it had often been in moments of happiness that I had become less guarded about my remarks or actions, and then, in my joy, I had disgraced myself. It occurred to me that Jem had told me what others thought of me, but not what he thought himself.

"I hope you know I am doing my best in the garden too," I said, humbly. "I sometimes wonder if you like me helping, or if you would prefer that I did not."

He glanced at me. "'Course I like it. There's always such a sight to do."

'Do you *really* like it?' I wanted to beg, but my father had taught me that asking for reassurance was vexing and not the mark of a man of character, so I said, in as confident and as final a tone as I could muster, "Well, that is all right then."

The breeze rustled in the tops of the trees and the water trickled on, an endless amicable conversation.

"Know what you're like?" Jem asked, suddenly.

"Do I know what I'm like?" I frowned. "I don't know what you mean."

"I'll tell you. You know that little old blackbird what comes when I dig in the garden? Keen, ain't he? Busy. And smart in his little black coat? Keeps me company, he do."

I could hear the smile in his voice. I had seen the bird often, sleek as silk. He had no fear of Jem and would hop to his feet, fossicking in the freshly turned soil.

"I'm like the blackbird?"

"That you are. I always look for him, like I always look for you. I'd be that sad if he ever stopped a-coming."

"He comes for the grubs and the worms," I said.

"Whyever he comes, he's welcome."

It was so unexpected and pleasing a comparison I could not help smiling. "I do wear black. And I do like to help you in the garden."

"See? You're a blackbird." His voice had been light-hearted and jocular, now he paused, and added in a different voice, "*My* blackbird. Aye. My little old blackbird. That's what you are." He sounded thoughtful, almost tender, as if he was saying something important that he had only just realised.

"Yes," I breathed.

I should have liked it above all things if it were true, if I really were a blackbird who could hop around Jem's feet all day and perch upon his spade handle when he stopped to mop his brow. Of course, I was only myself, but it felt as if Jem's fancy had lent to me a little of the blackbird's bright boldness, and I knew I should treasure his words forever.

Soon after this, I received a letter informing me that the bishop himself had requested that I present myself for an interview. I could barely describe the emotion with which these tidings overwhelmed me. What a morning I did pass! I scarcely knew what I said or did and was in a constant tremor.

When Lady Catherine drove by later that day, she stopped in the lane outside the rectory in her phaeton as she so often did, and I mentioned the matter to her. She informed me that His Grace was a cousin of hers by marriage, and that, as such, she had particularly asked him to take an interest in me. She told me I should be greatly honoured, for it was not every country clergyman who attracted the notice of the bishop, most men of my type having to content themselves with visitations from mere archdeacons or rural deans. She awaited only my gratitude.

I tried to express everything that was proper, and she drove away.

I stood by the gate for a long time, wringing my hands, and trying to convince myself that all would be well. Had I not met the bishop once before when he had instituted me at the church in Hunsford? It had been a solemn occasion, and I had been tongue-tied and nervous, but he had treated me kindly, afterwards speaking to me in an almost avuncular manner. Perhaps he might not find fault with me at this interview? He might even give me some good advice.

In any case, I could not refuse.

I was to travel, therefore, to Rochester, for His Grace was not at home in Bromley, but was busy with ecumenical matters. Usually, if I had to travel such a distance, I stayed somewhere overnight, for it was quite fifteen miles and would take the better part of the morning to get there and a good five hours to ride home.

I should have liked to take Jem, but the bishop's offices were much too close to the naval dockyards, and I would not have taken such a risk even if he had been willing. However, I did not want to be away from him overnight and since Pilot was no longer lame, and had not had any problems for weeks, I decided I should risk doing it all in a day.

On the morning of the interview, I arose very early, before dawn, and was well on my way by the time the sun came up over the horizon. I had been afraid of getting lost but found my way with ease, and arrived in good time, for Pilot had caught some of my unease and we had proceeded for much of the journey at a faster pace than usual.

His Grace received me in a small, wood-panelled room that could not have been his main office, but which felt like some sort of ante-chamber to that rarefied place. I was not sure what this meant, but his demeanour as we greeted each other was friendly and I decided he was trying to put me at my ease by making the whole thing quite informal. He was a handsome man, in his sixties or thereabouts, quite bald, with a well-modelled brow and a twinkle in his eye.

He invited me to sit and asked me how everything was in the parish. I perched on the edge of my chair and conjured Trafford, and attempted to give him the correct amount of detail. He then asked my opinion of how I was settling in and I told him I hoped that Lady Catherine and my parishioners alike found me assiduous in my duties as I was certainly doing my best.

He asked me then if I had any concerns or worries, and so kindly did he seem, and since I spent most of my days being concerned and worried—excepting, of course, the time I spent with Jem—that I cast Trafford aside and unburdened myself, with many apologies for troubling him. I wanted to tell him I was terrified always of doing or saying the wrong thing, but found myself, primarily, confessing how unworthy I felt to have been preferred by Lady Catherine over men more clever and more capable.

It cost me much to be so candid, especially with a superior, and I was afraid of his approbation, but he merely nodded and told me I must remember I was no longer plain Mr Collins, but was, since my ordination, a clergyman of the Church of England.

"You must not allow your natural humility to come overmuch to the fore, my boy. You must remember that the clerical office is equal in point of dignity with the highest rank in the kingdom, eh? So, bear up, Mr Collins, and behave as befits a representative of the Church and stop apologising. Do you understand?"

His advice struck me as a thunderbolt.

"But, surely, Your Grace, it would be wrong to omit to apologise when one has erred or inconvenienced another? Indeed, I have advised several of my parishioners so, and therefore feel I must not be remiss in my own behaviour. After all, does not the Bible say that if we do wrong we must repent, and if we do wrong seven times we must repent seven times?"

"Yes, yes, and I am sure your advice to your parishioners was sound. Do not trouble yourself on that account. But a man must take care not to further inconvenience the man he has inconvenienced by making his apology a burden to him. Must he?"

"No, Your Grace," I said, though I did not see how an apology could ever be a burden. Having been subject to many apologies of such extreme brevity that I had doubted the sincerity of the penitent, I felt the resultant doubt was more of a burden. Indeed, I should have liked many of the apologies I had received to have been more heartfelt and less brief. But perhaps there was an ideal length. Five minutes, perhaps, or ten. Or maybe the length of the apology should hinge upon the severity of the error or the inconvenience.

I would have liked to discuss all this with the bishop, but there were more important matters about my general behaviour and bearing that I wished to raise.

I said, "But with regard to the clerical office being equal in point of dignity with the highest rank; I'm sure your Grace is correct, and yet we all have our place in the world, do we not? I am not, in fact, equal to a duke. It would be impertinent to think so."

"You are somewhat too literal, my boy. Perhaps you are not equal to a duke, but he owes his allegiance to his God and his King, and you are a representative of the church, and as such it behooves you to behave with dignity."

"But surely I must remember my place?"

"Yes, and yet your place changed, Mr Collins, on the day you were ordained."

I detected, not exactly irritation, but a certain reserve, so I told him he had opened my eyes and that I should attempt to act upon his words and never to debase my office but to behave in a grave and stately manner while at the same time maintaining proper humility.

"Well, well, Mr Collins," he said, a little wearily, I thought, and soon after dismissed me.

I began my journey home feeling weary myself, not only because I had had an early start and a long ride, but because I now realised I had held high hopes of benefitting from the bishop's advice. Yet it seemed that his advice, like most advice, was no advice at all. I must apologise, but neither too much nor too little. But on when to be fulsome and when to be brief he had given me no guidance whatsoever. So, I was no better off.

I was to consider my office equal in point of dignity with the highest rank in the kingdom, and yet obviously I was not equal and so must remain humble. So how was I to comport myself? It must be as with apologising; sometimes I must be grand and stately and formal, and sometimes I must be meek. Yet with no guidance as to which role to adopt at which moment, I was no better off than before.

I frowned over these perplexing matters for a few miles, allowing Pilot his head, giving myself quite a megrim and seeing nothing of the beauties of the surrounding countryside. But then I remembered that if I got home before nightfall, Jem would be waiting in the garden to show me what he had done that day. My headache ebbed away, and soon I felt well enough to press my heels to Pilot's sides and to trot most of the rest of the way home.

# CHAPTER 7

It was the time of year when the dumbledores were dying when Lady Catherine raised again the subject of my marriage. I had the corpse of a bee in my pocket, wrapped in my handkerchief. I had picked it up on the walk to Rosings as it was a particularly large and beautiful specimen, and I wanted to show it to Jem as he had a particular fondness for the creatures. I was anxious not to squash it, nor to break its gossamer wings, and sat very carefully.

Although it had been cold overnight, it was stuffy in the drawing room and Lady Catherine was wielding a fan. I rather wished I had a fan myself, but such articles were not considered proper for gentlemen.

"Well, Mr Collins, and have you found a suitable young gentlewoman to marry?" She did not wait for my answer, but went on, fanning herself crossly. "You must make your proposal, sir, and stop this shilly-shallying. I declare, I do not know what is the matter with young men nowadays. They delay and delay as if the rest of us had nothing better to do."

Her mouth was pursed with discontent and her gaze rested upon Miss de Bourgh as she spoke, from which I surmised that a gentleman had been expected to make a proposal to that lady, but had not.

I was annoyed with myself for ignoring Lady Catherine's instructions, and, moreover, felt as if I had been caught out in some lie. I had been so taken up with Jem and with my duties that I had allowed myself to keep putting off this task for which I had such little heart.

"Indeed," I said apologetically, "It is not that I delay, Ma'am, for I would not delay my own happiness any more than I would risk your disapprobation. It is more that I have not, as yet, managed to locate a young lady who is both suitable and willing."

"Not located one? This is not to be borne! Why, there are fifty suitable girls in Hunsford alone."

There were around three-hundred-and-forty-eight people in the parish all told, though as they kept dying and being born and moving away and returning, it was difficult to be exact. However, a lot were men, and many were children or old people, or were married already. And while there were quite a lot of young unmarried females, many were unsuitable as potential wives for me, being from the lower orders. By my estimation there were around a dozen eligible young ladies in Hunsford, and yet Lady Catherine's estimation of fifty was so much higher that perhaps this was one of those situations in which I was not in possession of all the facts. If only I had not delayed in creating my lists of ladies 'Suitable', 'Unsuitable' and 'Neither Suitable Nor Unsuitable', I would know for a fact how many marriageable gentlewomen resided in the parish and would be able to proceed with the discussion in a sensible manner.

"I am displeased, Mr Collins." She snapped her fan closed. "You had but one simple task—and one moreover which will add greatly to your felicity and be of benefit to the parish—and yet you have signally failed to complete it. You could have been married for months by now."

I agreed, and apologised, and humbly submitted that I had been doing my best to discover a suitable young woman. Lady

Catherine tutted, and began to embroider upon the subject of her displeasure, continuing in this vein for several minutes. Clearly, this was no passing irritation, but a strong and lasting vexation.

I was sweating and my thoughts kept returning to the bee in my pocket, the delicate wings and the pleasing rotundness of its furred abdomen. I longed to scurry from the room and run to Jem and show it to him. Of course, I recognised the desire as a desperate longing for distraction from a task both dangerous and difficult: to wit, I must soothe her temper and give her hope that all should soon be as she wished it.

Presently, she paused, and feeling I must give her some optimism in the matter, I said, "Although, madam, as you so rightly point out, I have failed thus far in my mission, I do have some hope that I may soon add very greatly to my happiness."

Ladies do not snort, of course, but she made a sound that expressed some frustration, along with not a little disbelief. "Well? Explain yourself, sir. Who is she?"

I am no good at inventing on the spur of the moment and began to regret my last words. I attempted to call upon Trafford, but he could not help me here, for he would never have found himself in such a predicament and would have been married months ago. Yet I must say something. I opened my mouth. It would not have surprised me had found no words at all.

"Er...yes...yes..." I found myself saying. "Er...as your ladyship may remember, I am to inherit a small estate in Hertfordshire one day...er...that is, upon the death of one Mr Bennet, who was a relation of my father, may he rest in peace."

Even I had to admit that the words possessed something of the quality of the non sequitur. The thought had sprung to mind because Hertfordshire was approximately where I wished to be at that very moment. Also, perhaps, because some smaller, bolder part of me wished to remind her that while she had bestowed her beneficence on a mere curate with no connections and therefore was owed all my obedience and duty, had she *not* bestowed it, I would not always have remained in penury.

She frowned. "Of course I recall, for I have an excellent memory and am not given to forgetting matters whether they are great or trivial. What of it? Has the gentleman died?"

"No, no, Ma'am." I was glad to be able to answer a question without hesitation or prevarication. "I have received no information to suggest that such an unhappy event has taken place, and indeed I hope he may continue in good health for many a year."

"Well? What of him? Does he have a daughter?"

A flash of inspiration lit my mind, so bright I felt she must have seen it.

"Yes, yes, he does," I said, smiling a little with relief. "Indeed, while he has no sons, I understand that he has been blessed with several daughters. Four, certainly, and perhaps as many as five or six. And while I am not so privileged as to be familiar with their current matrimonial prospects, I do believe that with such a quantity of young ladies, there must be one who may be suitable to hear my addresses. For they must be gentlewomen surely?" Lady Catherine unbent sufficiently to bestow upon me a small nod, and, warming to my work, I went on. "And, moreover, gentlewomen, who, owing to their circumstances, have not been brought up too high but who will be able to make a small income go a good way. So, I am resolved to choose a wife from among them, so that on the death of their esteemed father the loss to them might be as little as possible when that melancholy event takes place."

Her brows lifted in surprise, but she nodded. "Your intention does you credit. Indeed, I wish all young men were as thoughtful when it came to entails. So, you are to visit Hertfordshire."

"I hope so, Ma'am."

"You hope so?" She snapped. "Why do you not go at once?"

"I have written to Mr Bennet." I blushed at the lie, though, of course, it would not be a lie a couple of hours hence, for I would write the letter this very evening and post it tomorrow. "I have proposed a visit, but good manners dictate that I may not arrive unannounced or uninvited, and so I am even now awaiting his response, which I sincerely hope may be favourable."

"I see."

"Of course, Ma'am, once I have received word from him, I may need to beg your ladyship's pardon as I must then quit Kent for a few days to travel and—"

"Two weeks, Mr Collins."

"I..."

"Two weeks is the correct length of time for you to stay with this Mr Bennet." She flicked her fan open again. "No more and no less. I hope that is what you have proposed in your letter?"

"Er, just so, Ma'am. That is exactly what I have done."

"Very good."

She spoke of other things, reminding me that I must be sure to ask Mr Chambers to cover my duties while I was away, for she would not have Mr Hay on account of his enthusiasm and the commensurate length of his sermons.

I was in a wonderful state of ambivalence, glad to have navigated such a tricky situation with aplomb, but already dreading my adventure to Hertfordshire, with all the attendant rigours of travel with a houseful of strangers at the end of them. No Jem. Unfamiliar food. Also, under the circumstances, how could the young lady do anything other than accept me, for she would certainly want to keep her home in her immediate family.

I had so hoped for at least another summer of freedom with Jem.

Perhaps I could insist upon a long engagement, or perhaps I could visit, make no proposal, and return to Lady Catherine with a tale of the unsuitability of said daughters. I could make them out as shrewish, or frivolous, or—but no, I could not impugn the reputations of the Misses Bennet, who were doubtless innocent and amiable young females. As Jem said, some lies would eat at one's heart.

My own heart ached. Yet I had known this day would come.

Had I not woken with a start in the small hours sometimes these past weeks, aware with every fibre of my being that I was disobeying Lady Catherine with my inaction? It had just been so easy to forget when I had slept again and woken to a bright summer's morning and a fresh boiled egg and Jem waiting to see what we should do that day.

Well, I must write to Mr Bennet that very evening, and then tomorrow I must drive with it to Pettiford, for I did not like to post it in Hunsford in case it got back to Lady Catherine that I had not sent the letter until after our conversation. I would take Jem with me to Pettiford on some excuse and apprise him of the situation on the way. Since all the unpleasantness lay at my feet, I would assure him that his position would be safe and that nothing would change between us, and then he would not be discomforted by the news.

As I left Rosings, I remembered the dumbledore in my pocket. I had almost certainly crushed it as I had forgotten about it during the difficult conversation with Lady Catherine. I removed my handkerchief from my pocket and opened it, intending to let the body of the insect fall to the grass. To my surprise, however, the creature stirred and arose from its shroud of white linen and soared into the air, wings glinting. Clearly, it had not been dead. Perhaps the warmth of my pocket had revived it.

I could not show it to Jem now, and yet, my spirits lifted along with the bee, for it seemed a small miracle.

The next day, as planned, Jem and I set off for Pettiford. I had said I needed him to help carry my purchases, which was perhaps not strictly necessary, but I had invented a need for more sermon paper, besides having my letter to post.

Mrs Fowke charged Jem with buying fish and a few other

necessary items for the kitchen that she could not get from the garden or the village. I promised George that we would also call at the apothecary since I had recently learned of a sovereign remedy for rheumatism, being nitre, sulphur and rhubarb mixed with treacle, and I had made a careful note of it, thinking it might help him.

The day was bright and 'finger cold' as Mrs Fowke termed it, being chilly enough to make the extremities tingle. Some of the hedgerows had already been cut, though some still harboured inky sloes and crimson hawthorn berries. The air smelled of woodsmoke and Pilot's ears were pricked as if he was glad to be out and moving.

I told Jem about my conversation with Lady Catherine and apprised him of the contents of my letter. Then I assured him in the sincerest of tones that nothing would change and that we should continue as we had these few months past.

He was silent for quite fifty yards, and then said, "Married?"

Usually, he was very quick, but I supposed had not been expecting the news. I explained again all the salient points of the matter, including that Lady Catherine had first raised the subject of my marriage in June, in fact, on the very day he had first arrived in Hunsford, and that while I had no personal wish to marry—rather the opposite—she expected it and would be most displeased if I did not carry out her wishes, and therefore, in a way, I did wish to marry as I did not wish to upset her.

"Aye," he said. "Lady Catherine. I see."

"It would be fitting for me as the rector to set the example of matrimony in the parish. It would bolster my role, so to speak. So, that would be a good thing. It would add to our security."

"You want an actress, not a wife," he muttered, snapping the reins, though Pilot was already walking along the lane with a good will.

"Yes, but I can scarcely advertise for that."

He was silent a moment, then said what seemed an oddly determined tone, "All right, but what about her, though, eh?"

"What do you mean? What about her?"

"Well, she thinks she's getting a husband when all you want is a...a...part."

"No, no," I shook my head. "Of course I'll be her husband. I will support her and be kind to her."

"Won't love her." He paused. "Or will you?"

I was stung at his implied criticism, for she would be getting the better part of the deal. "She will be the rector's wife. She will be respectable and want for little. I will make no unreasonable demands and will treat her always with courtesy. Many women would be glad of such a bargain."

"True enough." He was silent, guiding Pilot through the shallow ford in the Gadway. We should soon be out of the environs of Hunsford and on the Pettiford road. Then he said, "Still."

"Still, what?"

"Ain't it wrong to lie to the maid?"

"What lie?" My head was beginning to ache a little, as it never did usually when I was with Jem. "I will treat her with kindness and look after her always, as a husband should. And if she is decent and thoughtful and quiet about the house—you know, like Milly, or Mrs Fowke—then I am sure I shall esteem her most highly, as I do them."

He looked at me oddly, but said no more, and I was relieved to drop the subject and to speak of more interesting matters, such as the fact that one of the young apple trees had not one but three cankers, and whether it would be better to try to cure it or whether we should cut our losses and dig it out.

It was not until we had discharged our various duties in Pettiford and were halfway back to Hunsford that he said in a low voice, "You're resolved, then, to marry?"

His confusion bewildered me, for I had thought I had made it quite clear on the outward journey, but I explained all over again, and then once more, until I felt I was Obvious Collins indeed.

"But nothing will change, Jem," I assured him. "I promise. Your position in my household is assured."

"Aye, thank you."

His tone was oddly formal, but I again thought the matter at an end, when he muttered, "I'll lay some things will change, choose how."

I waited for him to elaborate but he did not, so I asked, "Which things do you mean?"

"You know," he said.

A spark of vexation lit in my belly for the situation I faced was difficult enough and while I had been trying all morning to school my apprehension, the dread of the ghastly adventure I should soon have to undertake was setting in: strangers to meet, unfamiliar food, dancing, and so on. I had no patience for guessing games, especially not with Jem, who was usually a refuge from such foolery.

"If I knew, I would not ask," I said, somewhat testily.

"You know," he said again, and then, as if realising how unhelpful this was, immediately added, "What we have been doing. Down by the brook. Frigging."

"Oh, that." We drove on, perhaps a quarter mile, while I tried to understand his reasoning. Eventually, I asked, "But why should that stop when I am married?"

He made an odd shrinking movement, like a horse twitching its skin to rid itself of a fly.

"Well...well...wouldn't be right, would it?" he said.

"Of course, what we do is a private thing. We both know that. We would not *tell* her. My wife, I mean."

"No, no. *Course* not. Don't mean that." He had gone bright red and appeared to be sweating, although it was not warm. In fact, a cold breeze had sprung up from the east. "I mean...if you're married...well, it'd be lying, wouldn't it, because you promise her. You say, 'forsaking all others' and you promise it. And so that's what she thinks you'll do."

"Others? But you're not 'others'. You're...you're...Jem. *My*

Jem. The marriage vows aren't...aren't..." I found my words dwindling away.

"Ain't talking about the likes of me?"

I was silent because that most horrid of sentiments—sudden realisation—was sweeping over me, laying bare a terrible landscape.

"But, Jem, it's not that I want to marry her, but I must pretend I do. I must say and do all the right things. Don't you see? So, can we not simply pretend about that too? It does not seem so very different."

"Don't know," he muttered, but a hundred yards later, he added, "*Is* different, though, ain't it? When we stay quiet about something we done, we both know it. Ain't no lie between us. You had a wife, *she* wouldn't know."

"But I have to lie, to get through life. I lie all the time, to everyone but you. I lie about what I want and what I like. I lie about who I am and what I believe. Because I must. And, lately, I have lied for you too, and for George and Milly and Mrs Fowke, because you are my folk and I love you and I wish us to all continue as we are for as long as I can contrive it, because the rectory is the only home I have ever had, and it is your home too, and theirs.

"And I do not know what Lady Catherine would do to us if she became truly angry with me. But I fear it. I fear it most terribly. She could, perhaps, not take the living from me without difficultly, yet even that she could do. She knows the bishop. He is her cousin by marriage, did I tell you? And there are other things she could do. Quiet words in certain quarters. A particular look when she speaks of me. She could turn the parish against me simply by driving past without waving her hand. I don't understand why that should be so, and yet it is. So, yes, I must tell lies to get through life, and I do my best to make sure nobody finds out they are being lied to, and I do my best to atone for my existence by doing my duty as best I can." I took a deep breath. "I thought you knew all this."

He pushed his hat back and scratched his hair furiously. "I *do* know. You *have* given me a home. You always were loyal. To a fault, maybe. But...a wife. I don't know. It's *different*, somehow. It *is*. It's some poor little maid as don't know nothing."

"She won't know nothing," I corrected. "She will have met me and I will be certain to describe Hunsford and the rectory in great detail so she may make as informed a decision as possible."

"Won't meet *you* though, will she? She'll meet the rector of Hunsford, what don't approve of novel-reading and what spends half his time thinking up compliments to Lady Catherine when he'd like to run a mile from the old besom."

My hand rose unbidden in alarm, as if to ward off a blow. "Jem! Dear me! You must never, *ever* say such things. You don't know who might be listening."

I peered around, but saw naught but fallow fields and a few rooks tumbling in the air.

"All right, all right." Jem said. "No one's listening or I wouldn't have said it. But you can't deny what I say is true. This Miss Bennet; she won't meet the real you."

I shuddered. "I should think not. Unless I am mistaken, she will be a well-brought-up young gentlewoman. She will have good commonsense and decided notions about what behaviours should be expected of a clergyman. I do not intend to disabuse her of those notions. Ever."

He was silent a long time. We crossed the ford in the Gadway again, approached Hunsford, drove through it, and then we could see George in the lane ahead, waiting to take Pilot, though doubtless it was paining him to do so.

"Have you got that bottle from the apothecary?" I asked Jem. "We must let George have it straight away."

"Aye." Jem said, patting his pocket. "I'll give it him. But anyway, since you're fixing on marrying, don't reckon we should linger after bathing any more. Even if you can, don't reckon I want to. Wouldn't be right. Wouldn't be able to look that little maid in the eye when she comes, that I wouldn't."

I wanted to argue, for his words showed he had understood nothing.

"But—" I started.

He cut me off, curtly. "Said my piece."

I had never heard him use such a brusque tone with anyone, least of all me.

"You're angry?" I said, but we had arrived and he was leaping down and greeting George. I climbed down myself and they led Pilot and the gig away, going together into a sphere of work where I was not welcome.

I went to my study and laid my new paper on the desk. It was a Thursday and I should be deciding upon the sermon for Sunday, but I could not settle to the work.

What Jem and I did together by the brook after bathing was pleasurable, but it was surely not that important. It was not as important as having him by my side, as knowing he was safe and well and slept warm and had enough to eat and that if anything happened to him—if he became ill or hurt—he should be looked after. But while usually I was simply happy when I thought of him, it now felt as if something was broken between us. It was plain he did not want me to marry, but wished everything to continue as before.

I threw down my book, put on my hat and took up my stick and went out again.

I knew not how I got there, but eventually I found myself stumbling up Hearse Hill, my heart in such a tumult I could barely catch my breath. That I must marry was plain. That I must not was just as clear.

I was now in a sloping field a couple of miles from Hunsford. I had been here with George once or twice, on our way back from seeing Mr Hay in Medbridge. I could not recall why we had come this way for it was not the most direct route to Hunsford.

There are no mountains in Kent, no crags or cliffs or dramatic vistas. Everywhere is gentle, with soft bucolic lines. But there are times one's heart craves a landscape that mirrors the upheaval within it, and this part of Hearse Hill was somehow expressive of great feeling due to the lake and the old stones that lay like fallen sentinels.

The great stones were seven in number. Such things were not uncommon in Kent and were often termed 'grey wethers' for they did resemble sheep from a distance. These ones were known as the Devil's Knucklebones, I supposed because of how they lay scattered upon the ground as if cast there by a giant hand. Why they were here, nobody knew. George had told me some folk said the fairies had set them here, and some the devil himself, but that a gentleman who was interested in antiquarian oddities had visited and said they marked the grave of some long-forgotten Kentish king, or maybe the Saxon chieftain Horsa, who might have given his name to Hearse Hill.

Not far from the stones, though divided from them by a thick hedgerow, lay the lake. It was not large, but was deep and held a sinister reputation. People said it was haunted and a boy had drowned there not long before I had come to Hunsford. It was called Hock's Hole.

I seated myself upon one of the cold knucklebones, the lichen crisp beneath my hand. Skeletons of Queen Anne's Lace brushed against my knees and I pushed back my hat to let the sweat dry upon my brow. I felt utterly weary. There was no right course of action. Whatever I did, someone would be annoyed with me.

I could stay here. I could not go back.

Evening would come and night would fall and the cold would enter me. I would shiver until my jaw ached. I would stretch out upon the stone and lie beneath the stars. Morning would come and then another night and so on until my coat grew lichen and birds carried away the threads of my stockings to line their nests, and I should not care for I should be away from the world.

Perhaps I did rest upon the grave of a king of old. He would have worn a wolfskin, perhaps, and never heard of Christ. He would have worried about the crops, his people, a foe named

Caesar. And all his kingdom now gone, and his people dead and his worries turned to ash.

Lady Catherine, if she wished, could make my life a misery. Besides, I owed her everything.

Jem loved me and was my friend, but my marriage would change things between us. He might leave me, which I could not bear.

No, but as the rector of Hunsford, and with Lady Catherine on my side, I was safe, or as safe as one ever is in this vale of tears. And if I was safe then so was Jem. Even if he left me, even if I could not bear it, I should always be able to help him. I could write him a letter, get him a good position anywhere he liked. I could give him money, if he would take it.

My way was clear. All the same I closed my eyes against it. I sat hunched, dry-eyed, and fancied the world wept about me.

So, I was to marry.

Well, then, I must choose carefully. Not for myself but for Jem and for Lady Catherine.

Lady Catherine would want her to be respectable, amiable, able to play quadrille and make up baskets for the sick. Jem would ask for nothing, but she must have no interest in gardening so that she would leave him alone, and then he might not leave. She must enjoy indoor pursuits; embroidery, reading and so on. Oh lord! But she must not bring one of those awful noisy pianofortes into the house. I could not bear it.

At the very edge of my hearing came a sound as of weeping. I glanced about but saw only the field and the hedgerow. It had likely been a sheep.

A musical wife would destroy my peace, but if she had all the qualities to satisfy Lady Catherine and to ignore Jem, then she should be my bride, though she played her blasted piano all the livelong day. If it kept her from making mischief in the garden, it would be worth it.

There. Again. Weeping, followed by a low moan.

It came from the lake. The haunted lake.

The hair prickled on the back of my neck.

I got to my feet, frowning. I did not believe in ghosts. Such things were rank superstition. I attempted to peer through the hedgerow, but it had not yet been cut and I could see nothing but leaves and branches. The weeping came again and I sidled along to find a better vantage point. Near to the gate that led to the lake was a place where the hawthorn grew thin.

There was a young lady on the shore, and she was no ghost. She was Miss Polkington, the eldest of four sisters, and from my parish besides. The Polkington girls had been on my Unsuitable list due to their tittering and their great quantity of aunts. Now, perhaps, I was feeling less fussy, but the family had recently been embroiled in the most terrible scandal. Miss Patricia, the youngest, had run off with a naval officer. That gentleman had deserted her somewhere in Bristol, and all reports told that she was now quite fallen.

I had little knowledge of female fashions, but usually Miss Polkington seemed a neat, well-turned-out young lady, indistinguishable from any other female of her class. It was difficult to see her clearly through the hedgerow, but currently she appeared to be wearing an old coat of her father's, which was over-large and gave her the appearance of a vagrant. She wiped her face with the sleeve and moved slowly along the lake shore, gathering stones and putting them in the coat pockets.

What could she want with such a quantity of stones? We had once conversed about gardening, for she was amiable enough, and she had vouchsafed to me that she was mad about ferns and had collected many varieties for her garden. Perhaps she was gathering more stones for her fernery.

Ah, but the scandal over Miss Patricia had changed Miss Polkington's own fortunes of late. Prior to the unpleasantness, Miss Polkington had had expectations of an offer from one Mr Barson, a respectable young man whose father farmed a good portion of land to the south of Hunsford. Miss Patricia's conduct had caused Mr Barson to withdraw. The Polkington girls were irrevocably tarnished by their sister's behaviour, and now must marry beneath them, if they married at all.

And all at once I knew why Miss Polkington was wearing her father's old coat and filling the pockets with stones by a lonely lake.

I hurried to the gate and approached her.

She did not notice me until I spoke. "Good day to you, Miss Polkington."

She started and turned. The soft skin about her eyes was swollen and her nose was red and shiny. Her bonnet had fallen back and her hair, which was so blonde as to be almost white, was in disarray. Her cheeks were a strange ashen colour.

"M...Mr...Collins." She reeled slightly, but was not so far gone that she neglected her curtsey.

"You are a long way from home, Miss Polkington."

She glanced about as if bewildered by this fact. "I suppose I am."

"Perhaps you will allow me to escort you home?"

"Oh. No. No. That is, no thank you, Mr Collins. I am...very well here, sir. Very well indeed."

She was trembling and although I saw her at church most Sundays I now noticed how thin were grown her wrists and how dark the circles beneath her puffy eyes. Her sister had ruined her chances with Mr Barson and she was suffering because of it.

"All the same, I think we should go now," I said. "It is getting late."

"I do not wish to go." She cast a glance at Hock's Hole. I did too. The breeze was whipping up wavelets that were grey at the tips and quite black beneath. Bottomless, they said it was.

"Your mother will be wondering where you are, will she not?" I asked.

Her mouth trembled. "No."

"I think she will," I said. "And your sisters. Your father, too."

"Let them wonder." Her mouth made a strange grimace. "It matters not."

"Miss Polkington, I hope you will forgive me, but you are a young lady and while your father may not object to your coming here alone, I think I would be remiss in my duty as your rector, and indeed, as a gentleman, if I allowed you to remain here unescorted."

"My father..." Her voice wavered on the word and she paused, closing her eyes briefly; I supposed against her feelings. "Father does not mind my walking alone." But she dropped the stone she was holding back onto the turf.

Matters hung in some kind of hideous balance and what I said next mattered more than words usually did.

Trafford had a dozen suitable remarks, principal of which was that if her father had been a little less permissive with his daughters, she might not now be labouring under the burden of shame and loss that had brought her to the cold lakeside. A burden, moreover, which would be loaded ten, nay, twenty-fold upon her family, were she to give in to her feelings and make fact the mortal sin she was contemplating.

A few months ago, I should have given voice to these sentiments, which were fitting and correct, the Church having clear commandments upon such matters. But while I had been Trafford a good deal of late, I had also been Master Willie, and sometimes Jem's Blackbird besides.

I knew, now, that sometimes a man may say what was in his heart, and it was not in me just then to lecture Miss Polkington about her father's failings or the additional shame she would visit upon her family if she killed herself. I felt, instead, that I should give her a way out of this ghastly situation in a manner which would allow her to retain her dignity.

"I think..." I spoke slowly and quietly, for I was not used trusting my impulses with any other than Jem, and my heart was beating fast. "I mean...when I first saw you, I thought that you were gathering stones for your fernery and I...I think that now you have enough."

"You don't understand," she said.

"I think I do."

"No. No!" She made an odd, unladylike gesture with both hands, as though she would shove me away, though she did not touch me.

I was somewhat vexed to be considered obtuse when I was merely trying to be tactful. I drew myself up. "Miss Polkington, I believe I *do* understand why you are here, but—"

"But you don't!"

"I don't really believe you are here to gather stones for your fernery."

"I know that! You said that to be kind. You *are* kind, sir. But I...I do not deserve it. You...you would not speak to me if you knew." She hung her head.

I was glad she thought I was being kind, but a familiar heaviness was settling over me for it was clear we were talking at cross-purposes. Still, she did not know I understood she was there to drown herself in the lake. Honestly, I despaired of making any person other than Jem understand me. I either pointed out matters that were too obvious, or I was so subtle as to have my meaning completely misunderstood. Well then, I must be obvious.

"I know why you are here," I said. "You want to drown yourself in the lake. But you must not, Miss Polkington. Indeed, you must not."

"It is better so, sir."

She was not without dignity as she said this, raising her chin and looking me in the eye. It occurred to me that I could offer to marry her now that Mr Barson would not have her. She would be grateful, perforce, and therefore humble and unlikely to cause trouble for Jem or to gainsay me in household matters. But Lady Catherine's horrified expression popped into my head. She would not consider any of the Polkington girls suitable for a clergyman's wife now. And, in any case, Miss Polkington's love of ferns could easily extend to vegetables. Besides, I had already posted the letter to Mr Bennet. Of course, I could not offer.

"No, no," I said. "I know you have been cruelly shamed and disappointed, but you are young, Miss Polkington, and will recover. If you will not think of yourself, please, I beg you, think of your family. Or of all the good works you might do. And some decent man may yet make you an offer. Of course it will not be Mr Barson, and it may indeed be someone you have heretofore considered beneath you, but, I ween, you—"

"You don't understand." She seemed to wilt. "I can never marry. I am wicked. I have had such sinful thoughts."

"Yes," I said, with what I felt was commendable patience. "Self-murder is a great evil. But you have not done it yet."

"No," she said. "It is not that."

I was lost. "Then what?"

"I...I..." Her face went red. "I wished her dead."

My confusion, if anything, grew greater. Who was she talking about? Had Mr Barson found another so soon? "Who?"

"Her. Patricia. My sister."

"Oh, I see!" I found myself smiling slightly in relief that we finally understood each other. She misunderstood.

"You think the situation amusing, sir?"

I stopped smiling. "Certainly not. Nothing could be further from my mind."

"You smiled."

"Only at your foolishness."

"Did you not hear me? I wished her dead. *Dead.* I wished that instead of running off with that awful, awful man, she had died. That's what I wished. That she had been kicked by a horse or died of a fever...and we...we would have mourned her and we would have buried her. And...Mr Barson...would have...have held my hand, perhaps, and been *sorry* for me and we would have been sad but then he would have married me, and we would have gone on with our lives, and instead everything is *ruined* and my sisters will likely never marry either and Mama spends all day in bed crying and will not eat and my aunts do not visit...and...do you not see?"

"You wished her dead. And you think that makes you so wicked that it would be better if you died too."

She frowned, as if hearing it so plain in the mouth of another made it suddenly less sensible, but she said, "Yes."

"I think you not so much wicked as logical."

A wave of colour crossed her face and she glared at me with an expression almost of horror. "Logical? *Logical*!"

"Yes. Your reasoning is quite sound."

"Sound! I am a monster. An unfeeling monster."

"You trouble yourself with what might have been, which I think is your true error. The past is not ours to rearrange and there can be no profit in doing so. But you are not a monster, Miss Polkington. You are quite right. Things would have been better for a great many people if Miss Patricia had died. It would have been a tragedy, certainly, but it would not have had such dire consequences. As it is, you and your family will suffer all your lives for your sister's transgression, and I expect she is suffering too. If we weigh all that suffering with the suffering you would have had if she had died, well, I think it is likely that her death would have been preferable."

She was staring at me, mouth ajar. She looked very silly, but of course I should not tell her so.

"If anything, you are to be commended, I think, Miss Polkington, for your clear-sighted view of the matter. It is not good to lie to oneself, is it?"

"I…no, sir?"

"No. So let us have no more of this 'monster' nonsense. You are just a young female who has had a disappointment, and a cruel one at that. But there is no need to drown yourself for wishing your sister dead. Indeed, I am sure that many in such a position might have wished the same. Instead, you must forgive yourself and resolve to make the best of things. Now, come, you do not really wish to carry all those stones all the way back to Hunsford, do you?"

She began to turn out her pockets. About half-way through

the job, she began to weep again, with such ferocity I thought all my arguments had been in vain. I said 'come, come' and 'there, there' and presently she ceased weeping and finished emptying her pockets. I gave her my handkerchief and she washed and dried her face at the edge of the lake. Then we set off for Hunsford.

I had a terrible headache from the strain and did not think I could bear to make conversation. However, with Herculean effort, I began to point out landmarks and to discuss the recent hop harvest and other suitable topics.

She said very little until we came to the lane which led to her father's house. Here she bade me farewell, and then, of a sudden, grabbed my hand and said, "Thank you, Mr Collins. God sent you to me today, I see that now. I will do as you have said, sir, and give thanks to Him my whole life and pray for my sister and do good works, sir. I promise it."

"Oh yes, God." I realised that I had omitted to mention him, which was surely a mistake. It was just so difficult to remember all the pertinent details when I was so exhausted and so heavy with the knowledge that Jem and I were no longer in such sympathy as we once had been. "Yes, yes. Excellent. God. Prayers. Good works. Very good, Miss Polkington."

"And I will pray for Mr Barson too," she added, in a low voice, "That he may make a good match soon and be happy."

She curtseyed and went off down the lane. I paused long enough to make a note in my little book regarding the likelihood of certain family members wishing errant sisters dead in such circumstances, and the advisability of a clergyman acknowledging that fact so that worse did not follow. Then, duty done, I plodded home to Jem.

I found him at the bottom of the nuttery field where he had been digging out a rotting stump. It was a big job and he had nearly finished. He must have worked hard all afternoon to do so much.

He leant on his spade when he saw me, pulling out his handkerchief and wiping his brow. The blackbird was at his feet, pert as ever, poking about for grubs. I had not known it was possible to be jealous of a bird.

"Are you still angry?" I asked.

He shook his head.

"It matters to you, though, doesn't it?" I said, "What we do by the brook."

"Don't it to you?"

"Yes, but I should rather forego it and know you were safe and well."

He sighed and leaned more heavily upon his spade. I had seldom seen him look so grave.

"I still don't see why we should forego it, though, just because I am married," I added. "I promise to do all in my power to ensure she is happy and comfortable. If she wishes to read novels or...collect ferns...or trim her bonnets, I shall not gainsay her such pleasures, so why should I gainsay myself?"

His eyebrows rose. "You're comparing what we do down there with collecting ferns?"

"Yes."

"Ain't really the same though, are they?"

"Aren't they?" I considered his point, but the more I thought about it, the more similar they seemed. Perhaps it was the detail that was confusing him. "I am not especially interested in ferns myself, it is true, but if I substitute 'growing potatoes' then I think the two are very similar."

"Growing potatoes." He was looking at me sideways, but I could see that somehow his mood had miraculously shifted. He was smiling, almost.

"Well, yes," I said. "Because both take place out of doors and both in your company. And both make me happy, and I think I should never grow tired of either. So, yes, I think them very comparable."

He gave a bark of laughter, after which he seemed unable to stop smiling and shaking his head. I smiled because he did.

He said, “You are a cure and no mistake.”

“I am only telling the truth.”

“Aye, I know. Come here. Come closer.”

I did as he said, though I hoped he would not try to touch me, for the nuttery hedgerow had been cut and we were visible from the road if anyone rode past. However, he kept his hands on his spade, and said in a low voice, “I don’t like this marrying business, but you must do as you see fit and then we shall have to see. And I hope as how you will still be my Blackbird after, but if it don’t seem right when all’s said and done we shall have to think again. Do you see?”

“You are making no promises,” I said, my heart sinking again. “Maybe we can go on as before, even if I am married, but maybe not.”

“That’s the way of it.”

He jerked his spade out of the ground, and began to hack away again. I watched for a while, then turned away, my nose full of the scents of earth and wood and rot.

# CHAPTER 8

I grabbed my hat and left Longbourn apace. I could not bear to be tittered at or questioned a moment longer. No, nor even observed. I hastened up the driveway and along the lane, going the opposite way to Meryton, for I had no wish to speak to anyone. Everything was drear and damp, but I was hot with embarrassment.

Miss Elizabeth would not have me.

Not even though I was respectable and comfortable, with a powerful patroness. Not even though, one day, Longbourn would be mine, and as my wife she could have been its mistress and kept her home, as could her mother and any of her sisters who were at that time still unmarried.

Did she not understand that now I would marry another woman? Likely one unknown to her, who would have no family feeling for Mrs Bennet, nor for Miss Bennet, nor Mary, Kitty or Lydia.

Of course, when Longbourn was mine, I would deal with any females then resident as charitably as I was able. I might even give them some regular income if that was a requirement to assure their comfort. But Miss Elizabeth could not know that.

Moreover, though she was pretty, she was not considered so comely as her sister Jane, and had been made no other offers, and might never attract any. Did she really have no apprehension of these facts? I could scarcely credit that she had refused me. I felt a fool, but she surely had no sense whatsoever.

I stopped in the middle of the lane. Could she indeed be playing some game, perhaps without even knowing she played it? I could bide my time, go back, ask her again after supper. Or play the game myself; leave Longbourn and let her believe I was gone for good. That would call her bluff. And then, a few months hence, I could return and ask her again.

My toes had gone numb with the cold. I walked on.

She was not playing a game. She had told me she was not.

The lane led down into a bleak and leafless wood, then uphill to a modest prospect of farmland. I did not know the area, but spied the start of a well-trodden bridleway which led off to the west, back through the wood. I took it, walking faster and my toes began to thaw.

There was a spiderweb, jewelled with dew. There, a hawthorn's scarlet hips, miraculously missed by squirrels and birds. A russet carpet of leaves lay beneath the trees and everywhere there was a rich scent like Mrs Fowke's good plum cake. I swung my stick and strode along, spirits rising. I might find some interesting new plant to tell Jem about. Perhaps I could collect an unfamiliar seedpod and we could sow it come spring and find out what it was. Today was Wednesday and I had only today, Thursday and Friday to endure. Early on Saturday I would leave this place and be back home on Sunday. My heart leapt at the thought and did not come back down to earth.

I found myself smiling. Yes, at the idea that I would see Jem soon, but there was something more. It took me another half mile to identify it as relief. Pure relief that Miss Elizabeth had said no.

I imagined the scenes had she said yes. I should have had to stay in the house, to receive congratulations and to show my new fiancée all the correct attentions. And she would have thought I truly wanted to marry her. I shuddered as I walked. I had persuaded myself that such deception did not matter to me, but suddenly, now I had escaped it, I could see it would have been cruel. All of Jem's misgivings had been so insightful and so sensible. I could hardly credit how light I had made of them.

As it was, I was reprieved, at least for a while. I could go back to Lady Catherine and tell her, honestly, that I had proposed to a very suitable young female and had been refused. Lady Catherine might think I should have done better, but I could pretend I was not happy either. I could play the part of the lovelorn swain, and if I played it well enough, I might win myself some months or even years of reprieve, for did not young men sometimes feel strongly in affairs of the heart and wait years for their beloveds to accept their proposals? I would tell Lady Catherine that I believed Miss Elizabeth's sentiments towards me would soften if I gave her time, and meanwhile wrote to her several times a week.

The bridleway led in a long curve and came back to the lane to the west of Longbourn. I was growing tired and hungry. I should get back and find Mr Bennet in his library, make conversation for half an hour or so and then it would be time for tea.

I was almost back at the house when I perceived a female figure coming out of the front door and proceeding towards me along the driveway. It was Miss Lucas, one of Miss Elizabeth's friends, and I could not avoid her.

"Ah, Miss Lucas." I bowed and lifted my hat. "Good morning."

"Good morning, Mr Collins."

She was a plain woman with a large nose and she was looking at me so closely I guessed she was wondering what to say. She would hardly be so ill-mannered as to raise the subject of my proposal and her friend's refusal, but all the same, to demonstrate that I was quite calm and wished to speak of other things, I enquired after her health, and then the health of her mother and father, and her brothers and sisters, of which she had several. She assured me she was well and they were well and I lifted my hat again to indicate that I wished to begin making my farewells.

"Will you walk with me in the garden, sir?" she asked. "It is not raining, for once."

"Forgive me, Miss Lucas, I was on my way inside."

"Yes." She took a deep breath. "To tell you the truth, they are still in a to-do. Mrs Bennet is speaking with Lizzie again and while Lizzie says very little, Mrs Bennet says enough for several people and that rather loudly. Come with me, do, sir, for you will get little peace inside."

"Well, well," I said. "But I expect it is quiet enough in Mr Bennet's study. I hope you will excuse me, Miss Lucas, I am rather tired, having been out walking this past hour." I lifted my hat, bowed, and took a step towards the threshold. "Good day to you."

"Mr Collins."

"Miss Lucas?" My voice sounded weary. I turned back. I had not meant to be ill-mannered but I had talked enough. Conversation with strangers was ever a chore and I had done so much of it lately.

"I hope you will permit me to tell you how much I have enjoyed hearing you speak of Hunsford and your garden and the rectory there. It sounds quite charming, and all, really, that any sensible person could want."

My weariness receded somewhat. "Thank you, Miss Lucas. You are quite right. The rectory at Hunsford is most commodious."

"It certainly sounds everything *I* should want in a home, sir."

It came to me that she was being kind, and that, perhaps, she wished to distance herself from the opinions of Miss Elizabeth, who had not been swayed by my descriptions of Hunsford.

"Then you are a young lady of good sense."

"Yes, it is just the sort of place I should like to live. The rector of Hunsford's wife should want for nothing, I fancy, having an excellent house, a respectable position, and plenty of opportunity for gainful employment and good works. I am an active, capable sort of woman, Mr Collins, and I like to imagine myself in a place where I may prove useful." She paused, and then added, "Useful to my husband, you understand, sir, should I ever be fortunate enough to receive a proposal. I should prove a dutiful wife, I think, having a quiet disposition and a good understanding of the benefits of household economy."

"Your sentiments do you credit, I am sure," I said. "You will doubtless make someone an excellent wife one day."

"Thank you, sir."

She coloured slightly. Perhaps she felt it had been indelicate to discuss matters pertaining to matrimony when I had so recently been disappointed.

"I will go in now, if you will excuse me," I said.

"Of course." She curtseyed. "I will come in with you. I am to spend the day here, did you know? I hope we may speak again later. Lydia and Kitty were speaking just now of walking to Meryton this afternoon and perhaps I shall go with them if you will accompany us? I should be very glad of your company."

In truth, I was glad to have a course of action suggested to me as I was unclear about my role as disappointed suitor, and had been wondering whether it would be most fitting to pursue the unattractive course of refusing luncheon and stopping in my chamber for the afternoon. Clearly, Miss Lucas did not think that kind of behaviour was necessary, and she seemed a sensible sort of female. I could not imagine her suggesting an outing that would be thought unfitting for a man in my position.

I bowed. "I should be very glad to oblige you, Miss Lucas. Assuming it does not rain, that is, as I have only one pair of shoes with me and I should not like to get them wet. It was an oversight on my part, I confess. I should have considered the time of year. Of course, I have the dress shoes I wore to the ball but I can scarcely wear those about the place."

"I quite understand, sir." She curtseyed again. "I have not

been much away from home myself, but I understand it can be difficult to know just what to bring. But assuming the weather remains fine this afternoon, I shall look forward to our walk and to talking with you further about Hunsford and your situation there."

I wished her good day again in the hall and made for the study, where I hoped Mr Bennett would not be in possession of the best chair, for if I was walking to Meryton in the afternoon I should certainly want a rest between now and then. However, Mr Bennet was very much in evidence, ensconced in the good chair with a large folio. I felt a spurt of irritation, unwarranted, of course, for it was his house and his library. I greeted him politely and asked after his health.

"What a very punctilious young man you are, Mr Collins," he said. "For you have not failed to enquire most minutely about my health every day you have been here. Indeed, one might almost think you had a particular interest in the matter."

"Thank you, sir," I said. "Certainly, I believe that it is only by showing great attention to the correct behaviour that we may assure ourselves of never giving offense. And it is surely the duty of a guest to concern himself with the health of his host."

"Interesting that you raise the topic of giving offense, sir. For some might say that a man in your position would do well to allow himself to become—shall we say, a little more disinterested —in the health of a man in my position."

How I loathed talking to Mr Bennet! He bewildered me at every turn. And yet he seemed to enjoy doing so and it was my duty to converse with him. How I missed Jem. How I missed talking with him of potatoes, or cabbages, or the best way to deal with slugs or with wayward parishioners. I never felt he was trying to trick or to confuse me. His conversation was plain, like a piece of good bread when one is hungry.

"Might they?" I answered, valiantly trying to imagine what type of person might hold such a view. "It sounds unmannerly to me. For does Saint Luke not say 'as ye would that men should do to you, do ye also to them likewise'?"

"He does, sir. He does. Yet the Bible also says we should season our words with salt, does it not?"

"Colossians," I said. "One should speak with grace, seasoned with salt."

"Quite so, Mr Collins. Quite so. The salt is the thing, eh? It adds a little interest, does it not?"

"You are quite right, I'm sure, sir," I said, desperately. I had no idea what we were talking about.

There was a pause and then he said, in a musing way, "So Lizzie will not have you, Mr Collins."

This was the last thing I wished to discuss, but the dictates of good manners meant I could not remain silent. I managed to say, "No, sir."

"Females are empty-headed creatures, though Lizzie, perhaps, is less empty-headed than some. Perhaps you are better off without her?"

"I should not say so," I said, with some dignity, and, I felt, gallantry. "Though I own that I do not understand her."

"I should think not! For how could an educated man such as yourself understand a girl such as Lizzie?"

I had the strongest feeling he was somehow laughing at me, though I could not see *how* and what he said was, I could see, a fair point.

"I flatter myself that I try to understand the thoughts and the concerns of my flock," I said. "For such understanding is part of the duty of a clergyman. I therefore make many observations of their behaviour, and some of them are young ladies with little formal education. I could name Miss Polkington and her sisters, for example. I realise you are not personally acquainted with these ladies, but I can assure you that there are many similarities between them and your own daughters, and I think I understand them quite well."

"Ah, sir, you may depend upon it that where girls are

concerned you do not truly understand them, but merely think you do." He was half laughing in a sly sort of way that I thought most inappropriate under the circumstances.

I tried to understand his joke, but humour is often bewildering to me. It so often seems to consist of pointing out something the jester believes is obvious, which does not seem at all obvious to me. Or it consists of crowing over the misfortunes of another. I will never, for the life of me, understand why seeing a man slip and fall in the mud should be the stuff of merriment. So, I could not cap his joke, yet I must say something, for such were the rules of conversation. Eventually, I decided it would be best merely to restate my purpose at Longbourn, in case it had slipped his mind.

"Well, sir, I came here to try to make amends to your daughters, due to the entail which means I will likely be the means of doing them injury one day. Of course, one could argue that *I* am not the means. The means is the law. But I am the result of that law personified and therefore I felt it was only right that I should extend the olive branch and do my best to—"

"Yes, yes, yes, Mr Collins. I am aware of all that, for you put it in your letter. Let us not speak of it any longer, for I suspect the disappointments in this matter have been many and experienced on all sides, and I do not believe it is good for the constitution to dwell overmuch upon such matters."

He was capricious indeed to raise a topic and then say he did not wish to speak of it. But perhaps I was the one who had erred. Perhaps he had wished to glean fresh information on the matter, and here I was, being Obvious Collins again.

"As you wish, sir." I said, humbly. "I only spoke of the matter because it appeared that you wished to. For myself I would be glad to let it alone."

"Very well, then Mr Collins." He cast me a look that, oddly, I felt was not unkind, and murmured, almost to himself. "After all, you are very young."

I felt I should correct him upon that matter, for I was five-

and-twenty, but he had returned to his folio and to speak now would be to interrupt him.

I picked up a book of sermons and let my gaze drift unseeing across the lines of text and dreamed of Jem, and of the summer's day he had first led me to the pool, and I tried to imagine next summer, with everything just as it had been—myself unmarried, Jem and I free to spend time together.

If only I could push the image of Lady Catherine's frowning eyebrows out of my idyll. Surely, she would understand that I had been disappointed in love and must spend some time mending my heart and waiting for the young lady to experience a change in hers. It was a scenario that seemed perfectly sensible, and quite the sort of situation that occurred often in life.

At luncheon I found myself seated between Miss Kitty and Miss Lucas. To my relief, Kitty was taken up with her sister Lydia, but Miss Lucas asked several intelligent questions about Hunsford.

I would have enjoyed the conversation more had I not been so preoccupied with thoughts of Lady Catherine's displeasure at my failure. Yet, after all, I *had* proposed, and I *had* been refused and Lady Catherine could not object to my retreating for a time to lick my wounds before starting the search for a new young lady. Surely her displeasure would be with the situation and not with me?

After lunch, the walk to Meryton was proposed by Lydia and Kitty. Miss Lucas appealed to me again to join them, and since it was not raining, I felt able to oblige. On the way, Miss Lucas dawdled somewhat, which was not like her, and we kept falling behind the two younger girls. I had to keep exhorting her to hurry for it would not have been fitting to allow two young females to go on unescorted when I was present.

We did not linger long in Meryton, for we discovered that most of the militia officers were gone off on some manoeuvre, and after the girls had made their duty to their aunt and visited a milliner's establishment to look at ribbons, we set off home.

Miss Lucas again seemed to walk more slowly than usual. I enquired if she was tired and she said she was, a little, though generally she believed herself a very energetic person.

Kitty and Lydia were, by now, distant figures, arm in arm in the lane ahead. They could come to little harm on the way home and I shortened my stride to match that of Miss Lucas. She was asking if we had such-and-such a plant in the vicinity of Hunsford, whether fumitory or vetch grew in our hedgerows, and if we had much eglantine. I answered with alacrity for it pleased me to speak of plants. She moved onto apples and asked whether I had a certain variety of cooking apple that did well in the Longbourn orchard and which was excellent for pies and dumplings. So my head was full of apples when she asked, "Do you like children, Mr Collins?"

I shrugged. "I cannot answer, for children are as diverse in their characters and manners as the members of any large grouping of humanity. If they are gentle and kind then I suppose I must like them, but if they are thoughtless and cruel then I do not."

Her eyebrows rose and I realised, with a sinking heart, that Trafford would have answered quite differently, with a hearty, "of course!" and something about blessings.

"Of course," I stammered, endeavouring to get back onto firm ground. "We must be fruitful and multiply and fill the earth."

"Yes," she said slowly, but something had sparked in her eyes and she was looking at me closely. She smiled. "I do believe you are an honest man, Mr Collins, to answer me as you have."

"No, no," I said, alarmed. "I mean, of course I flatter myself that I am honest. Indeed, it is my duty. But what I mean is that I abide by the teachings of the church."

"Of course, sir."

"Do you like children, Miss Lucas?" I asked a little wildly, for I felt I had erred in the conversation.

She smiled. "I find them easier to forgive than adults, in any case, for if they are thoughtless, it is only because they know no better."

I gave some polite answer, while privately thinking that often children knew better but chose to behave badly anyway, but she went on in a curiously determined tone of voice, as if she had made up her mind to something.

"If I were married, I would, of course, do my duty by my husband and give him children if I could, but you gave me an honest answer just now, sir, so I will also observe that I am the eldest of seven and there is a five-year difference between me and my sister Maria who is the next oldest. That means that as the eldest girl I have played nursemaid to my little brothers and sisters for twenty years, and while I love them as a sister should, were I not blessed with children myself I think I should not be terribly sad but would find much to occupy my time. In short, sir, I should be glad to sit down sometimes and to read or sew or write letters without interruption. But perhaps you think me hard-hearted, or do not believe what I say?"

"It is common knowledge that women desire children," I said. "But I have observed that while most mothers appear to take much pleasure from the company of their progeny, there are a great many who appear to find them very tiresome, and while they would not like any misfortune to befall them, are glad to see them only seldom and do not miss them overmuch when they are not there."

"I think you are right, sir."

She appeared to be attempting to suppress a smile. I wasn't sure why, so I added, with dignity,

"You may ask how I have formed this view, Miss Lucas, not being married myself, but as a clergyman I have visited the homes of a great many people of all types, in Sussex and in London, where I held curacies, and of course, now, in Kent, as the rector, and I have watched my parishioners closely. Indeed, I have often taken notes as to their behaviour. And while I do not think there are many women who would go so far as to say they regretted having children, there are some who very much regretted it, and there are a considerable number who would be content with seeing their children but half a dozen times a year." I thought about this, and added, "Or, certainly, seeing *some* of their children very seldom."

"Certainly, sir, I think Mrs Bennet finds some of her daughters to be easier company than others," she said.

"I'm sure they are all very accomplished and amiable young ladies," I said, because this is the sort of gallant lie I have found goes down well.

"But some, perhaps, with more sense than others," she said.

"Anyway, Mrs Bennet strikes me as a woman of good sense and I'm sure is a good model to them. She is ever cognisant of the future and does what she can to ameliorate its uncertainties. To me that seems the most sensible approach to life, especially in these terrible times of change and conflict."

"Certainly, she thinks more often of the future than does Mr Bennet." Miss Lucas remarked. Then she sighed. "I think often to the future myself."

I told her such forethought did her credit, and alluded to the parable of the wise and foolish virgins. This brought us back to Longbourn where I must, of necessity, be much in the company of Miss Elizabeth.

I was unsure how to behave towards her. I could not be too sanguine for I did not want her to deduce I was relieved she had refused me, a situation that must surely be offensive to any young lady. The safest approach seemed to be to scarcely ever speak to her, and so I took refuge in what I flatter myself was a rather stately formality.

Luckily, Miss Lucas still seemed much inclined to seek out my company and so we spoke of her clever method for growing mustard and cress, and my opinions, borrowed, I must own, from George, on sowing carrots, and on the cunning use of human hair in keeping deer away from one's garden.

That night I went to bed quite calm and slept almost immediately. I woke, however, in the early hours with a jolt. The disappointed presence of Lady Catherine had hovered over me all yesterday. Now, in the dark of the night, it was as if her spectre pounced, bringing with it all the dread of her displeasure.

I rehearsed again my arguments. I had located a suitable young lady. I had paid her all the correct attentions—conversing with her, dancing with her, complimenting her and so on. I had made my proposal very properly. I had done everything Lady Catherine could have asked of me. It was not my fault the lady had refused me. Surely, Lady Catherine would see that? But the ache in my gut and the iron bar inside my shoulders said otherwise. Lady Catherine would find fault, for had I been more personable, or displayed less of my true character, then likely Miss Elizabeth would have accepted me.

For a day I had been able to pretend to myself that Jem and I might have another untroubled summer together. Now I could not persuade myself that this would be the case. Lady Catherine might give me a week's respite, or even a month or two, but then she would start badgering again and she would never give up.

Ah, but how often had I lain in such a torment, only to discover that the horrors I had imagined did not come to pass? Consider, for example, how afraid I had been of telling her I had taken on a second man to help George. I had not slept for days —but when I had given her the news, she had barely blinked. Of course I must marry eventually, but perhaps Jem and I *would* get another summer?

Ah, but summer was seven months away, and while that might seem but a moment to me, to Lady Catherine it would seem I dragged my heels for an eternity—

Round and round my thoughts turned, first to one scenario, then to the other. I lay as one paralysed while the grey November morning came and young Molly brought hot water and made up the fire.

The household began to stir. There were women's voices on the stairs and the sound of the pianoforte, and, presently, the aroma of ham and of tea. Yet still I lay there, my mind running hither and thither like a rabbit pursued by a hound.

Molly came again, tapping at the door, bobbing a curtsey and asking, "Beg pardon, sir, but Mrs Bennet asks if you would like breakfast in your room this morning, sir?"

"No, thank you, Molly. I will get up."

"Yes, sir." She shivered. "Ooh, it's cold in here, sir. Shall I make up the fire again before you get up?" She did not wait for an answer but proceeded to stir it to a goodly blaze. She went to the jug and touched it. "Cold. I'll fetch you some fresh hot, sir."

"Thank you, Molly." Her kindness had brought me out of my ghastly fugue state. "What a good girl you are."

She coloured and bobbed. "Thank you, sir. Ain't nothing but what the mistress would expect."

She was right, perhaps, but all the same I made a mental note to leave her an extra tip on my departure.

Despite the dreadful start, the day passed rather quickly. The young ladies of the family had departed for Meryton by the time I came down and so I was left to eat my breakfast in the company of Mrs Bennet, who was sympathy itself and who soon became quite animated upon the subject of her daughter Mary and what a quiet, biddable, amiable girl she was. I was glad to converse upon any subject that was not Miss Elizabeth and, in any case, Mrs Bennet was easy company for she talked enough for two people and all I must do was to nod and agree from time to time.

Later, the girls arrived home and a letter came for Miss Bennet from Miss Bingley. The Bingleys, I gathered, had quit Netherfield Hall. Miss Bennet seemed not much distressed by this news, but from Mrs Bennet's reaction I guessed that one of the gentlemen from the Hall—though whether Mr Bingley or Mr Darcy I did not know—was the one she had been expecting to make an offer for Jane. It was hard on the poor lady to have had hopes of seeing both her eldest daughters settled, and to find that neither were. But, as she said, the Bingleys would be back.

To my great relief we were to dine with the Lucases and departed to Lucas Hall in the middle of the afternoon. Miss Lucas approached me as soon as we arrived with the express intention of showing me some seed catalogues and I spent quite an enjoyable afternoon with her in the perusal of these delightful publications.

After dinner, while the others talked or drank port, or played some rowdy game, I found myself seated near the fireside with Miss Lucas. Lady Lucas and Mrs Bennet were nearby, but so deep in conversation it was clear they did not notice our presence.

"Tomorrow is your last day with us, sir." Miss Lucas spoke quietly enough, but her tone, I felt, had steel in it. She had been friendliness itself at dinner, and I could not think what I could have done to earn her displeasure, so I merely agreed.

"In an hour or two you will be going back to Longbourn with the Bennets and I may not see you again for—well—I do not know when I may see you again," she observed.

"Alas," I said. "That is true."

A silence fell between us, though what with the crackle of the fire, and the whistling of the wind outside, and the chatter and laughter from the gamesters—chiefly from Lydia and Kitty—and the matronly murmur from the ladies on the other side of the fire, it felt quite comfortable, until, that is, Miss Lucas burst out, "Mr Collins, I…I must speak," and immediately fell silent again.

I waited for her to do just that, but she did not. The fire crackled. Kitty shrieked something about fish.

Feeling that words of encouragement were perhaps expected of me, I said, "Then please do speak, Miss Lucas, for I have enjoyed your conversation these last few days and I am sure you have something of interest to impart."

"There is something I wish to say, but I am concerned that you may think me unmannerly. Or, perhaps, forward."

"Oh." I sat back a little in alarm. "Then perhaps it would be better to read aloud."

"I...I wish to speak to you of...of business, sir."

"Business?" Her father had been in business before his elevation. Perhaps she wished to speak of that. I said as much, and added, "But I'm afraid I know nothing of business, Miss Lucas. I am a clergyman, as you know."

"Even a clergyman must look to his interests though, must he not, Mr Collins? To ensure his lands are well managed and his parishioners give him the tithes which are due to him and so on."

"That is so." I was beginning to feel as I felt when talking to Mr Bennet. If she went on in this manner, I should make my excuses and join Sir William and Mr Bennet at their port and I scarcely wished to do that. I shifted in my seat. Only one more day to get through and I could go home.

"Mr Collins." Her voice was very low and I had to bend to hear. "This is the business I wish to discuss: You, I think, are in want of a wife, and...and I am in want of a husband, and I wish you to know that were you to honour me with a proposal, I should not say no and indeed should think myself the most fortunate person in Hertfordshire."

I would have sprung to my feet but the only thing that would move was my eyebrows, which I felt were somewhere near my hairline.

Lady Lucas, perhaps sensing that I had received some kind of shock, said, "Are you quite well there, sir? Is the fire spitting?"

"No, no," I said. "I am quite well, thank you, Lady Lucas. It is an excellent fire."

"Good, good. I am much relieved." She turned back to her conversation with Mrs Bennet.

Miss Lucas was staring into the flames, her eyes overbright and her colour very high. Trafford was waiting in the wings and I drew myself up and rehearsed his line about begging her pardon but thinking I now had nothing more to say to her. Then I should withdraw—to the gentlemen and the port, or to Longbourn, which was not far from Lucas Hall.

"I...I..." I managed, and then fell silent. For while what she had said was beyond the bounds of decency, the part about my being in want of a wife was also, regrettably, true.

"I...I am not sure I want a wife after all," I said. It was both true and untrue.

Her colour grew higher, but she spoke very calmly and with dignity. "I know I am not handsome and have no dowry."

"Oh, no. Truly it is nothing to do with your appearance. Or your situation."

"You are kind, sir, but all the same it is the truth." She took a deep breath and went on in a determined tone. "I am seven-and-twenty and I would not stay here to be a burden and an embarrassment to my family if I can help it. In return, I will be the most dutiful wife for which a man could ask. I will put your happiness first in everything. I will visit the sick and the poor and the dying and so assist you in your duties in a manner befitting the wife of a rector. I will teach the children of the farm labourers to read their Bibles. If you want no change to your household, then there shall be none. I shall discharge the duties you give me, and take on none that you do not. I will not bother you or fuss, but will take what is offered to me and count myself fortunate."

I frowned, for she had in a few short sentences, described almost exactly what I wanted in a wife. "You would grow discontented, I think."

"I would not, sir." She spoke with such calm that I was almost persuaded. "I would remain ever grateful to you, as you remain grateful to your patroness."

I shifted. "I would not want you to live in fear."

She glanced my way. "Oh. I see. Of course." To my great relief, she turned back to the fire. "I would not live in fear, sir. You may be many things, but you are not a tyrant. Indeed, I think you try always to be kind. Your coming to Longbourn was motivated by kindness, was it not? So, if I wished to follow some course of action, I would consult you, and if you had objections, you would explain them to me, honestly, and then I should understand and should not do anything to put your security and happiness at risk."

"Or the security and happiness of my household," I added, because that, really, was the greater consideration.

"Of course." She glanced at me again, this time with a look that I saw more usually in persons from the lower orders. I might have been confused by it, but she went on, "Your care for your household elevates you, sir, and I respect you the more for it."

A glow that was not from the fire warmed my cheeks. A few months ago, I would have proposed to her that instant, in gratitude for her kind words. But these days I was not quite so unaccustomed to praise or affection, having heard such sentiments quite recently from Jem.

"Your suggestion has come as a shock, Miss Lucas."

She smiled, ruefully. "So I understand, but I hope you will not dismiss it out of hand." She glanced at me again, and added, more timidly, "You do not appear to be dismissing it."

"I do not wish to give you false hope, Miss Lucas, but I am not dismissing it immediately."

"Thank you, sir. You are very good to consider it."

"Miss Lucas, you may as well know that I am looking for a wife because Lady Catherine has indicated in the strongest terms that she wishes me to do so."

My words were out of my mouth before I could stop them. It was as if her candid and open manner, albeit shocking, had called to my own natural tendency to honesty. She did not fail me, but met me at once.

"But it is not something you want for yourself." Her manner was matter of fact and she did not sound surprised.

"It was not my idea," I allowed.

"You are not like most other men, are you, Mr Collins?"

A cold thread of fear ran up my back. I had gone too far, allowed her to see too much of me.

"No, you're mistaken," I said, censoriously. "I am very like them. After all, many men are not much fond of the company of females and many men never marry."

"You are quite right, sir. I beg your pardon. And if we were to marry, I would understand if we did not spend much time together." She paused, then said in a voice so low I barely heard, "Indeed, if we lived together more as brother and sister than husband and wife, I would accept that without question."

She fell silent, which was a relief, for she had given me much to think about. Almost everything she had said was improper, and I could not bring a woman so heedless of the bounds of propriety into my household. One could not tell what such a person might take it into her head to do. She had said that, if we married, she would ask me before following any course of action, but how could I know she would hold to that? It was true she did not strike me as a flighty kind of female, but I had known her less than a fortnight and was not disposed to trust her on such a short acquaintance.

However, from the outside, and setting apart the scandalous behaviour of this evening, she was quite respectable. She was generally polite and sensible. She was capable and of an acceptable age. Her father was decent and amiable and could be introduced to Lady Catherine without concern. Miss Lucas was, in short, almost exactly the kind of woman Lady Catherine would find suitable.

"Do you play quadrille?" I asked.

She looked a little startled, but answered calmly, "Yes, sir. I used to play with my grandmother."

So that was a mark in her favour. I tried to think of more questions that would be pertinent to the topic, but what she had said about living together as brother and sister kept ringing in my ears. But why was I even attempting to question her? The very fact she should make such scandalous offers meant I could never accept them. I should do as Trafford would, and withdraw at once.

Yet I did not, but continued sitting there beside her, while the flames danced and the wind outside brought a rattle of rain against the windows and my heart pounded with the possibility she had set before me, and what it might mean, for me, and for Jem.

# CHAPTER 9

To my amazement, that night I slept almost as soon as my head hit the pillow.

I dreamt of Jem. We were walking the streets of Oxford, where I had been so miserable, but in the dream it was bright morning and we were happy. Some disturbance came from behind us—I had neglected to perform some important duty that I had not known was expected of me. Someone furious was behind us, but whether it was my father, or Lady Catherine, or Jem's brother Jack, or an angry bursar, I did not know.

Jem grabbed my arm and we ran, but we were not afraid. We were laughing. We knew we should get away. The streets vanished and we were transported as if by magic to Butler's coppice, which in turn transformed into the place behind the raspberry bushes in my father's garden. Jem pulled me into a green and secret nook and we lay there panting, laughing, ferns dancing over our heads. We were safe. He was warm and everything good and I pressed myself against him and my pleasure woke me in the dark of the best spare bedroom of Longbourn.

I mopped up with the handkerchief which I had placed beneath my pillow and lay down again. I would rinse it tomorrow in the ewer and no one the wiser. My body was limp and my mind so lucid that the darkness seemed as velvet, soft and friendly, and my way lay before me, bright as the beam of a candle.

Presently, Molly came in, made up the fire and poured hot water into the ewer. She had barely closed the door when I sprang out of bed. I splashed my face and hands, rinsed my handkerchief and laid it over the jug to dry, dressed and put on my shoes. I crept downstairs. The front door was barred, but it was also locked. I had not expected that and rattled the handle uselessly.

"Oh, sir, was you wishful to go out?"

Molly's voice made me jump, even as I realised it was her.

"Yes," I said. "I want a walk. By myself. Do you have the key?"

"No, sir. Mr Bennet keeps it."

"I must get out."

"Do you come the back way, sir."

She led me down the narrow corridor that led to the kitchen. From inside came the thumping of dough. Mrs Hill must be making her breakfast rolls. I did not want to speak to anyone, and had indeed lifted a hand to touch Molly's arm to tell her so, when she ducked about a corner to the right and then immediately to the left. Here was a narrow door, and a full chamber pot waiting like a cat that wishes to go out.

"Beg pardon, sir," Molly said, covering the chamber pot with a duster.

"No, no, it is quite all right. Thank you, Molly. Er...I shall be back later."

Outside it was barely light and very cold. I turned my coat collar up and strode to Lucas Hall, icy clouds of breath parting in the air before me. In my frenzy to be out of Longbourn and on my way, I had not considered that Lucas Hall would also still be closed up for the night. But thus it was, with most of the rooms presenting blank curtain linings, very white. I could hardly go banging on the door, for I did not want anyone to know of my presence beyond she who had brought me here. I had certain questions to ask of her and certain demands to make. How she answered would determine my next course of action.

I must, perforce, wait. It was too cold to stand still so I marched up and down the lane. At any other time, I should have felt awkward and might have thought the better of my plan and walked back to Longbourn. Today, with my dream of Jem buoying my determination, I strode with the confidence of a militia officer.

I turned smartly on my heel and did the same thing all over again, noting with interest that moving with such resolve was heightening my feelings of bravery. I took out my little book and made a note of this discovery for occasions that required courage in the future, such as dinner parties at Rosings or meetings with the bishop.

I had marched up and down exactly seven times when I spied a curtain twitching in an upstairs room. The pale face of Miss Lucas appeared for a moment. She lifted her hand in recognition and motioned to me that she would come down. The curtain closed again.

I continued my marching, and had completed the journey past Lucas Hall and back twelve times when I turned to find Miss Lucas approaching me, clad in a blue pelisse and a yellow bonnet.

"Good morning, Miss Lucas." I doffed my hat and bowed.

"Mr Collins." She curtseyed. She looked tired and paler than usual and I guessed sleep had eluded her.

"I have considered everything you said yestereve," I said, then realised this was not strictly true because I had fallen asleep and had therefore not given her offer nearly as much thought as I would have expected. "Or, most of what you said."

"Thank you, sir."

"I have some questions, if you will permit them?"

"Of course, sir. I should be glad to answer."

"Good. Firstly, do you sing much? As you go about the house?"

She looked startled, but said, "I don't, I suppose. I could sing if you wished it."

"No, no. I ask because I cannot abide it. It is very distracting to me, singing."

"Then there is no problem, sir, for generally I sing only in church, or sometimes in the evenings if father asks for a song."

"What about the pianoforte? Do you play?"

"I can play a little and would soon improve with practice."

"No, no. There is no piano at the rectory and I do not wish for one. I find music very disturbing. As with singing, it is so difficult to ignore, and in my own house I want peace, not racket."

"Then I shall continue without singing overmuch, sir, and will happily allow my piano practice to lapse."

"We have spoken much of plants and seeds. But I wish to make it clear that the garden at Hunsford is my domain. I do not want you bothering the men, nor giving them instructions which may conflict with mine."

"I understand, sir, and should be glad to leave that to you."

"Good. What else? Ah, yes, this is important: Lady Catherine is my esteemed patroness and must be treated as such. No word of criticism will pass your lips. Not even in private. And you will pay her every courtesy that is due to her age and rank."

"Yes, sir. I would in any case behave thus. But I give you my solemn promise."

"And...and what you said about living more as brother and sister than husband and wife. You meant that?"

"I did, sir. If you wish it."

"Yes, but will people not talk? If you do not have children?"

She shrugged. "It is not unknown for marriages to be without issue. Generally, people are sympathetic to such a plight."

"But might it not cast doubt upon the marriage?"

"I do not think so, but if you wished you might tell people

that I was in a particular situation, and then, a few weeks later, put it about that that was no longer the case. Such things happen, you know."

"That is true." I nodded. "Well, then. I...er..."

Deep down, perhaps, I had expected her to say that she could not be content unless she began every day with a merry sing-song, or that she must needs have a pianoforte or die, or that to instruct the men was her deepest desire. But she had agreed with my every wish, and so calmly and with what seemed complete sincerity.

I found it harder to draw breath and, despite the chill air, sweaty heat prickled out beneath my arms and down my spine. My hands trembled. I recognised the signs well. I was about to embark on a course of action that involved some risk. I was about to ask her to marry me.

But what if she had only agreed to everything now to secure her position? What if, once we were married, she made all kinds of demands upon my person and my patience, because I could hardly set her aside. I had a brief, nightmarish vision of myself, cowering in my study as she ordered Jem about and turned George away as a useless old man, and replaced Milly with some smart London hoyden. My imagination took me further and I saw myself curled upon the rug beneath my desk, hands over my ears in agony as she sang and played the piano for hours. And visitors would adore it and compliment me on my wonderful musical wife and I should have to agree.

"Miss Lucas."

"Mr Collins?"

"You say all these things now, but how can I know you will not have a change of heart? What if you have a sudden longing for a pianoforte? Or children?"

"Well, sir. Perhaps my best answer is to give you my demands, as you have given me yours."

"Demands?" I echoed, becoming truly alarmed, for surely that was not part of the bargain? "Oh, but...but..."

"Come, Mr Collins," she said briskly. "In business, both sides must state their case, must they not? Yes, I am in want of a husband, or, rather, I am in want of as pleasant and as secure a future as I can acquire and I consider this the best way to go about it. But I remind you, sir, that you are in want of a wife—and not just any wife as it turns out, but a very particular kind of wife that I do not think you would be able to find just anywhere. I can be the wife you want. I can do everything you have said, and willingly, but you must also extend some courtesies to me."

I was afraid I had fallen into a trap and said nothing.

She said, in a gentler voice, "I think you will find that what I want is not so very difficult, sir. Indeed, I think my demands may align with your own wishes."

"Well?" My voice quavered.

"I wish that I might have a room of my own besides my bedchamber. A morning room, perhaps, that you do not use overmuch, or a small parlour."

"There is a parlour you might use," I said. "But what would you do in there?"

"I should read, sir, and sew, and write my letters, and enjoy being alone and mistress of my own house. Which brings me to my next demand. I will be as frugal as you wish, and cross my letters and turn the sheets, but I would like a special allowance for books. Five pounds a year, sir, if you please."

Books would keep her well away from Jem and I was inclined to agree, but I recalled some of the reading material I had seen about the place at Longbourn. "But you must not read anything a rector's wife should not read."

She shook her head. "I must be allowed to choose freely, but if I buy any volumes that could be considered unsuitable, I will keep them in plain covers and hide them behind other books and never speak of them."

This seemed fair, and sensible. "Very well. What else?"

"Nothing else."

"Nothing?"

"I hope you will allow me to visit my family sometimes?"

"Of course! You must visit them as often as you like."

She nodded. Her colour was high but she looked determined. "Very well then, sir. I have said everything I have to say. It remains only for you to ask me—you know—the question, if you wish to do so."

"Yes. But first, may I ask you—not because it will change matters, but simply because I am curious—Miss Elizabeth is your friend, is she not? Will it not cause difficulties between you, if you accept a suitor she has rejected?"

She took a deep breath. "Difficulties? I would not go so far as to use that word, sir. She will be surprised, it is true, but she is young and beautiful and still hopes to marry for love. She does not dwell overmuch on the practicalities of life, as I must." She paused, then said, in a rush, "And while she is my friend, my *dear* friend, it was not ever thus. She is seven years my junior. Once, I had friends my own age. Three of them. But they are all married now, and two have gone away and one has five children and I see her very seldom. I made friends with Jane and Lizzie when I was twenty and they were girls of thirteen and fourteen, because otherwise I should have had no one outside of my own family to talk to. Perhaps you have little conception, sir, of what it is to be a young woman who sees her friends married about her while she remains unwed. But that is what happened to me."

She wiped away a tear. I was terrified she would start weeping, and had she done so I might have retreated in confusion, but instead she shrugged and gave a half-laugh, as if to say 'you see what fools life makes of us?'

She was, of course, nothing like Jem. She was narrow where he was broad, slight where he loomed. She spoke very differently and had the dainty mannerisms of a female of her class. But all the same, at that moment there was something about her that reminded me of him.

Perhaps it was her honesty, which was quite without self-pity, perhaps her air of diffidence, which I guessed cloaked an unconventionality of outlook so well that it would go unnoticed by all but the closest observer. Some of my nervousness fell away and, perhaps for the first time during this whole adventure, I could truly see a future in which all would be well between me and the three most important people in my life, to wit, Jem, Lady Catherine, and my future wife.

"Miss Lucas, I should like to make myself clear: I have set out my stipulations and you have set out yours and all has been agreed, but I...well...I suppose I should also like us to be as...as friends, if that would be possible. We shall have to appear as husband and wife in public, of course, but privately, also. My household is quiet and harmonious and I like it that way. I hope that just because I have set down some rules, you will not feel that I will ever treat you with anything less than the most tender civility and generosity. I want you to live in contentment, truly, I do."

"Thank you, sir." She curtseyed. "It's kind of you to say so, and I'm sure we will be friends."

"Good," I said. "Then we shall all be happy."

She smiled for the first time that morning, her tired face suddenly appearing lighter and younger. "Do you know, sir, I think we will be."

I found myself imagining the ruminations she must have been prey to during the long watches of the previous night. After all, had I been a different sort of man, I might have made all kinds of difficulties for her. I might have carried report of her behaviour to her father, or to Mrs Bennet. I might have got up this morning and gone to say a few stern words about her conduct to her vicar. Or, last night, I might have gone into Meryton and entered the inn that was frequented by the militia officers and made her into a figure of fun with them. She would have certainly considered these sorts of possibilities herself, and yet she had still acted. She was admirable, really, to have been so bold.

"And I should like to acknowledge, Miss Lucas, that you have been most uncommonly brave these past couple of days. Not many young women would have been courageous enough to say to me what you have said. You took a risk, did you not?"

"I did, sir." She smiled again, and I thought I could see true warmth in her eyes. "But it was a calculated one. I feel I may now tell you that I have watched you very carefully this past fortnight, and it soon became obvious to me that, if left to yourself, you would never behave in a mean or ungentlemanly manner. You might have been shocked at my proposal, and you might have refused to speak with me, but I think, in the end, you would not have made trouble for me and would simply have gone home. You dislike strife and confrontation, I believe."

"That is true," I said.

"And, moreover," she went on, still smiling, "I have another confession to make. It is this: I questioned the Longbourn servants about your habits and behaviours. Yes, I spoke with young Molly. And Mrs Hill. And with John, the gardener. You will be happy to hear that all gave excellent reports of your thoughtfulness and interest and politeness. And I do believe, sir, that it is in how a man conducts himself with people of that type that one may judge him best. No, my risk was not so great."

I asked her, then, to marry me.

She accepted.

We shook hands to seal the bargain and after a few more words about how we should arrange matters and how we should conduct ourselves, we parted.

# CHAPTER 10

I spent the journey home in a lather of exhausted nerves. Lady Catherine, I was almost sure, would approve of Miss Lucas, but it was Jem's reaction that had my stomach churning and my thoughts racing, for I felt the situation could go either way with him. Hope is ever one of the most difficult sentiments to endure, for the apprehension, that sense of balancing upon a knife's edge, is utterly wearying. I had to keep reminding myself in the sternest tones that hope was a thousand times better than the morass of gloom into which I should have sunk had Miss Elizabeth accepted me, for she was surely just the kind of innocent young maiden that Jem had been so keen for me to avoid.

I did not get home until late on Sunday as the roads had been bad about Sevenoaks due to heavy rain. Mrs Fowke met me at the door, let me into the warm, took my coat and assured me all was well. The house smelled of beeswax and apple-wood fires and I could have embraced her, though of course I did not. She led me to the dining room and set out one of her hearty veal and ham pies, to which I could not do justice, blaming my lack of appetite on the indignities of travel. As soon as I could, I repaired to my study. I sat in one of the easy chairs before the fire and asked her to send Jem to me, saying I wished to enquire about the crop of white filberts which he would have got in while I was away.

He came, and I saw him for a moment as a stranger such as Mr Bennet or Miss Elizabeth might have seen him; a big, rather ill-favoured and common-looking country fellow, dressed decently enough, for he was wearing the brown striped velvet waistcoat which was his Sunday best, but with nothing interesting nor remarkable about him.

Then I blinked and he was my Jem, and it was so wonderful to be with him I could not stop smiling, even though I knew I should not, for our coming interview might not go well and then such happiness would seem ridiculous, and possibly even importunate.

"Welcome home," he said.

"Oh, Jem, how I missed you!" I stood up, the better to see him. "You have no idea how glad I am to be back."

"You wanted to know about the filberts?"

"Yes! How many—no. The filberts were an excuse so Mrs Fowke would fetch you. I have news."

"You're getting wed."

His tone was clipped. He was standing with his arms crossed, face angled slightly towards the fire so that he was looking at me out of the corners of his eyes. It seemed a sullen pose, or a defensive one.

"Yes, but, Jem, I hope you will not be angry. Indeed, I hope you will be pleased with me, because she is very practical, and is seven-and-twenty, and labours under no illusions. We made an agreement and it is a very sensible one, I think. I told her everything—well, of course not *everything*, but I was as honest as...as decency allowed. I told her I must marry because my patroness desires it although I do not, and we agreed we would be friends, and she said she does not mind whether she has children, but wishes to have an allowance of five pounds a year to spend on books, to which I agreed. And she promises she will not interfere in the garden, nor make any alteration to the household, nor will she ask for a pianoforte, nor sing unless necessary. And she can play quadrille and...and...of course I understand that you may wish to reserve judgement until you have met her, but I think you will see that she does not expect anything of me that I cannot give her, and is content with that. More than content. She wished to marry. She is happy, I believe, with our bargain."

I felt I was babbling, over-explaining, but he did not move or speak.

"Oh, and Jem! I did the wrong thing at first and proposed to one of Mr Bennet's daughters who—thank goodness!— refused me. Had she accepted, it would have been everything you said would be wrong because she is young and pretty and hoping for love and you were right. It would have been very wrong. So I had a lucky escape. And I have thought of you every moment and wished you could see everything in the Longbourn garden. I have brought you some seed potatoes from Mr Bennet's gardener which are a different variety and I think you will like them. They are very hardy and have a very good texture when boiled which we both agree is so important, don't we? And I have collected some other seeds for you, besides, and I hope you are not angry and will think I have done well. Oh, and her name is Charlotte. Miss Lucas." I was wringing my hands together in my anxiety, but I could not seem to stop. "Please say something."

He opened his mouth, then closed it like a trap. He seemed to considering everything I had said.

"You really told her? All that? You didn't want to marry but had to?" There was an accusatory note to his voice which I felt I did not deserve.

"Yes. I told her I must marry because of my patroness." My voice sounded timid, even to me. I tried to inject some reassurance into my tone. "She was very understanding."

He gave a short laugh. "Wonder she didn't slap you."

"Oh no." I was quite shocked, for he had clearly got the wrong idea about what sort of person she was if he thought she would behave in such a way. "She is kind, I think, and has excellent manners, though she is plain and has no money. She did not wish to become an old maid. Well, or an older one. Her father is very respectable."

He was squinting rather. "Wait. First you asked one maid, and she said no, so you turned about and asked the other?"

"Yes, yes, and you are the first person I've told. I didn't mention it to Mrs Fowke because I wanted you to hear it from me."

"How long then, between you asking the first and asking the second?"

"Er..." It seemed such an extraneous detail, but it must be important to Jem or he would not ask. I attempted to calculate and found I was too nervous to do so properly. "A few days. Two or three. Does it matter?"

He smiled, and hope leapt within me, warm and alive.

"No," he said. "Just...just..." He shook his head, still smiling. "You are a wonder, sometimes. How you manage things. Don't reckon there's many men as could do what you just done." He sat down, rather suddenly, and to my surprise, in one of the chairs in front of the fire. "So, you told her true, this Miss Lucas. Well, if that don't beat all!"

"Is it all right for you to sit there?" I seated myself in the chair opposite. "What if Mrs Fowke comes back in?"

"She comes back, I'll get up." He was still shaking his head. "Blimey, Blackbird, did you really do it? Well, I always did think as how you were honest to a fault usually. When's the wedding?"

He had called me Blackbird and something tense and taut in me eased. All would be well, now, surely? "As soon as possible. Early January."

He sat back in his chair, staring into the fire. "So, you told her. All fair and square."

I sat back myself, suddenly so weary I cared not if Mrs Fowke came in and saw us sitting there together like friends. In fact, if she came, I would suggest we all had a glass of madeira wine to celebrate my upcoming nuptials. We had some, for I had got in several bottles for Mr Chambers and other such callers. But Mrs Fowke did not come and I let my gaze linger upon Jem.

How strange was life that it could be so relentlessly harsh and bewildering, and yet it could also give one moments like this. My Jem, safe and warm and well-fed and clothed, sitting by the fire with me while the east wind blew icy outside, and he was smiling at me with something like admiration and there was no spot nor stain of disharmony between us. My chest ached with such tender feeling that I longed to give back to him some little part of the contentment he gave me.

"You see, Jem, everything will be all right," I kept my voice down, for I still expected Mrs Fowke at any moment. "I am not free to live as I please, but I will always find a way to look after you, no matter what happens. I'll always be your...your..." But I did not know what to call myself in relation to him. I was his friend, certainly, but somehow that did not feel warm enough. Eventually, I said, simply. "I'll always be yours. Always."

"Aye, I see that now. In it together, ain't we? Forever." He wiped his eye with his knuckle and sniffed. "Luckiest day of my life, I reckon, the day I met you behind those raspberry canes."

"The luckiest of mine, too," I said.

He made my heart swell, sitting there with the firelight illuminating his face and playing over his brown velvet waistcoat. Everything about him was marvellous, every feature so beloved that I wished the moment could last forever.

"I wish we could sit together like this every evening." I said. "It is too cold, nowadays, to linger out of doors or to go down to the wilderness."

"Spring'll come again. Then summer."

He was right, but I had to make sure that this meant what I guessed it meant. "So, we'll go down to the brook together again one day? We'll bathe? And afterwards, if you want to, you'll let me watch?"

"'Course. All those things. First warm day."

"Perhaps we may get a warm enough day in March or April?"

He grinned, likely at my wishful thinking, for April was generally far too cold for bathing or lingering out of doors. "We may."

"I wish there was somewhere we could go in winter."

He shook his head. "Thought on that plenty myself."

"You couldn't think of anywhere?"

"Stables, maybe. But George is in and out, unless he's laid up. And it ain't just him. Remember the time Mr Hay came calling and put his mare in the stable hisself because he knew George had been bad and the mare had had a cough?"

I nodded. That was the problem with anywhere around the rectory. People came and went: Boys with messages that I was wanted somewhere, the churchwarden on parish business, the clerk, the sexton, women wanting churching, men wanting charity, Mr Butler's Tess with a brace of woodcock or a trout, not to mention Mr Chambers, who seemed to stop in every week for a glass of something on his way home from whatever ghastly sport with which he had seen fit to entertain himself.

Jem and I could, perhaps, find a moment to ourselves in the barn, or the woodshed, or concealed behind the gig in the tack room, but it would always be risky, and inside the house would be even more perilous. Mrs Fowke and Milly generally knocked and waited for my call before entering the study if they knew I was in there, but there had been times when they had thought I had gone out and had simply tapped and entered immediately.

In any case, that they knew everything that went on in the house I had no doubt. Servants generally did. It would take but a moment's inattention, a forgotten duster, a sudden decision to wash a particular window and Jem and I would be discovered, and then what might happen I did not dare to think. Perhaps they would tell no one, do nothing, but what if that were not the case? It did not bear thinking about.

In any case, the very idea of creeping around at night and furtive meetings and hastily buttoned breeches made me almost ill from tension. I expect there are men who can put their fear of discovery aside for long enough to take their pleasure, but I am not of that type. What I wanted was to lie at my ease with Jem in the ferns, for us to speak of whatever we wished without fear of being overheard, and to be certain that none could observe us.

"I would invite you to my chamber at night," I said. "But I do not dare. There would be no pleasure in it, for I would always be awaiting discovery."

"I know." He nodded. "Ain't worth the risk."

"Spring," I said. "Celandines and violets, primroses and irises."

"Lords and ladies," he added, nodding. "Hellebores."

"Bluebells."

"Dog's mercury, wild garlic."

"It won't be so long," I said.

"I will have met her by then." He sounded thoughtful. "You sure she don't want children?"

"She said she did not mind. She has several younger brothers and sisters and has played nursemaid to them all her life. She says she would be happy to spend some time in her own company."

He nodded, and was silent a time, then said, "She changes her mind and wants them, you give her them, you hear me?"

He sounded so determined, I did not argue nor restate the lady's case, but simply said. "I hear you."

"Good." He stood up. "I better go. I'll tell them in the kitchen, eh? They'll want to wish you happy."

I stood up too. "I'll tell them myself, and ask Mrs Fowke to pour us all a glass of wine."

He reached for me suddenly and took my hand.

We were standing still before the fire but it felt like the last time he had held me, as he led me to the pool. It was as if he were about to take me somewhere beautiful, somewhere free, a place where I need neither dissemble nor strive to be anything other than myself; a place where I was loved.

"Aye, reckon we've got something to celebrate," he said.

THE END

# ABOUT THE AUTHOR

Lee Welch lives in Wellington, New Zealand with her family, two cats and a dog. She likes escapist fantasies, long walks in the hills and reading children's books in bed.

### A message from Lee

Thanks for buying this book! If you liked this story, please remember that book reviews, mentions on social media etc help indie authors like me to keep writing. So, if you can spare a few moments to review, recommend or talk about this book – thank you! – Lee

### Connect

Sign up for my infrequent newsletter: https://leewelchwriter.com/newsletter/
For occasional blog posts: https://leewelchwriter.com/
Facebook: https://www.facebook.com/leewelchwriter/
Bluesky: @leewelchwriter.bsky.social
Instagram: leewelchwriter
Twitter: @leewelchwriter

# ACKNOWLEDGMENTS

A huge thank you to everyone who helped me with this book!

Editor: May Peterson at www.maypetersonbooks.com

My marvellous beta readers: Sol Vera, Scott, AJ Demas and Jackie North.

My family, who put up with me when I'm writing—and when I'm not.

And special thanks to all my wonderful readers and social media followers and friends. I hope you enjoyed this book!

**More m/m romance by Lee Welch**

- Seducing the Sorcerer (also available as an audiobook)
- Salt Magic, Skin Magic (also available as an audiobook)
- Mended with Gold.

Printed in Dunstable, United Kingdom

76567089R00088